THEIR BORDER TEMPTRESS

Men of the Border Lands 3

Marla Monroe

MENAGE EVERLASTING

Siren Publishing, Inc.
www.SirenPublishing.com

A SIREN PUBLISHING BOOK
IMPRINT: Ménage Everlasting

THEIR BORDER LANDS TEMPTRESS
Copyright © 2012 by Marla Monroe

ISBN-10: 1-61926-608-3
ISBN-13: 978-1-61926-608-7

First Printing: January 2012

Cover design by Les Byerley
All art and logo copyright © 2012 by Siren Publishing, Inc.

ALL RIGHTS RESERVED: This literary work may not be reproduced or transmitted in any form or by any means, including electronic or photographic reproduction, in whole or in part, without express written permission.

All characters and events in this book are fictitious. Any resemblance to actual persons living or dead is strictly coincidental.

Printed in the U.S.A.

PUBLISHER
Siren Publishing, Inc.
www.SirenPublishing.com

THEIR BORDER LANDS TEMPTRESS

Men of the Border Lands 3

MARLA MONROE
Copyright © 2012

Chapter One

"What the hell?" Brice slammed on the brakes and skidded to a stop not three feet from a downed buck in the middle of the road.

"Brice, there's a truck off in the ditch over here. I bet it lost control when it hit that deer." Garrett, his best friend, poured out of the cab and raced to check on the driver.

Brice threw the truck into park and got out to check that the deer was dead. He figured by the size of it that it had done some damage to the truck that hit it. The driver would be lucky to be alive. He slid down the bank of the ditch to the sounds of his friend cursing a blue streak.

"Fuck, Brice. It's a female."

"How bad is she?" Brice braced himself for the worst.

As a paramedic before the year of catastrophes, he was used to seeing the damage a car wreck could do to a human body. He didn't want to see it on a female. There were so few left of them now, they were bought and sold like cattle on the black market.

"I can't get to her. We've got to get the door open. It looks like the deer hit her on this side, and she lost control and ran into the ditch. She's got a head injury for sure by the way she's bleeding."

"Okay, let's work on this door," Brice said.

They pried on the door until it gave and Garrett was able to get it open enough that Brice managed to squeeze in to check her over. She had a two-inch cut at the edge of her scalp that was bleeding like crazy. Blood covered her face, making it difficult to tell if she had any facial injuries as well.

"Garrett, get the first aid kit and hand me some gauze and tape so I can stop this bleeding."

He heard Garrett climbing up the ditch. He returned to check out the unconscious female and found she had a swollen left wrist. He'd used his knife to cut her seat belt and slit her clothing, so he could check her chest for bruising from the steering wheel. Thank God there was none around her chest, but the left side of her ribcage was reddened and beginning to bruise. More than likely the deer hitting the door had slammed her into it. He hoped there weren't any broken ribs.

"Here you go." Garrett handed Brice a handful of gauze and a strip of tape already cut.

"Good going." He gently applied the gauze then taped it securely around her head, adding enough pressure to slow down, if not completely stop, the bleeding.

He continued checking down her body. She had bruising all up and down the left side. He couldn't see much of the right side to know how badly she was hurt there. They needed to get her out and somewhere warm. It was the early part of October, but already the days were beginning to get chilly and the nights downright cold.

He hated to move her because he didn't know how badly she might be hurt internally, but there were no doctors or hospitals in the Border Lands, and she would die for sure if they left her in the car much longer. She needed what little medical attention he could give her.

"Got to move her. I'm going to need your help, Garrett."

"I'm here. Just tell me what to do."

"I'm going to lean her out the door so we can pull her straight out. You carry her to the truck once I get her legs off of the floorboard. Be careful of her ribs on the left side. I'm worried they're cracked, if not broken. She's bruised to hell back there."

They maneuvered her around in the truck and finally got her out so that Garrett could carry her up the steep embankment of the ditch. She began to squirm and moan in his arms.

"Brice, she's waking up, and she's not happy."

"Put her in the backseat, and I'll work on her there. Then see what she was carrying and load it in our truck while I'm settling her down."

"Put me down. Oh, God. What happened?"

Brice could hear the female fussing in a weak voice.

Garrett tried to soothe her as he carried her to their truck.

"Easy, there, little lady. You're hurt awful bad. Brice is going to see about you, though." He laid her in the back of the truck and backed away for him to get to her.

"Who are you? What are you doing to me?" she demanded.

"Shh, we're not going to hurt you. You hit a deer and had a wreck. We're just trying to help you."

"God, I hurt all over. My head." She moaned.

"Let me check your ribs now that I've got you so I can see you."

"You've taken my clothes off! What are you doing?"

Brice ignored her fussing and warded off a few weak blows from her right hand. Her left hand hung limply and was already swollen. He hoped it wasn't broken.

"You may have some busted ribs, and I think your left wrist is either broken or badly sprained."

"I've got to get home. I'll be okay when I get home. Everything will be fine once I'm home."

She sounded like she was going into shock now.

"Do you have someone at home who can take care of you?"

"It's just me. I'll be fine. Just take me home." She began to try to sit up.

"Don't move. If you have a broken rib, it might puncture a lung. I need to tape them, but I can't like you are now."

"Is the blasted deer dead?"

"Yep, it's dead all over." He didn't have a clue where this was going.

"Get it then and bring it with us. It'll make good meat for the winter. I can use all the meat I can get."

Brice stared at her as if she were crazy. Her head injury must have been worse than he thought. She had a good size knot on the outside, so he hadn't thought there would be swelling on the inside, but he could have been wrong.

"I moved what little she had into the back of our truck. I need to move the deer out of the way so we can get going." Garrett walked up to the truck and peeked in at the woman.

"She wants the deer."

"Huh?"

"She said she needs the deer meat. I can understand. Can you load it, or do you need help?"

"I can get it." He shook his head but walked over to the downed animal and began dragging it toward the back of the truck.

Brice picked up the female's head and climbed in the back with her, placing her head in his lap. He used another piece of gauze and began to clean some of the blood off of her face. Most of it had started to dry and wouldn't come off. He felt the back of the truck jerk. Then he heard the sound of the tailgate closing.

"Where to?" Garrett asked as he climbed into the cab.

"Drive straight up this road till you come to a crossroads. Go left and follow the curves around until you come to a big tree that's split. Take another left, and it will lead you up to my house."

Garrett followed her directions and Brice continued to check her eyes and the bleeding from the gash on her head. She kept talking about all the things she had to do when she got home, and he worried that her head injury was serious. He sure hoped the man who had her would be able to care for her. What in the hell was she doing out by herself anyway?

"Here we are, Brice. It's a beautiful house. Big." Garrett pulled up into the drive and parked under the carport.

"Let's get her inside."

"Did you get my pack?" the female asked.

"Uh, yeah. Why?" Garrett asked as he took her from Brice's arms.

"Key is in it."

"Hell, forgot to get the keys from the truck." Garrett cursed.

"You'll have to unlock the door," she said.

"I'm getting the keys," Brice told them.

"Your man isn't home?" No wonder she was out by herself, Brice thought.

"Don't have a man. It's just me. That's the way I like it."

"Ah, hell," Garrett muttered.

"Door's open." Brice held it open so Garrett could carry the female inside.

They walked in the door and she directed them left. They passed into the living room, where Brice could tell she'd been sleeping on the couch in front of the fireplace. It was probably the best way for her to stay warm without a man to share her bed.

"You can't stay on the couch with these ribs. Where is the master bedroom?" Brice asked.

"Upstairs. Put me down, and I'll walk. I'm too heavy to carry up there."

"You don't weigh much of nothing." Garrett took the stairs without hesitating.

Brice grinned. He knew Garrett was strong and could handle her. He would have been able to carry her up, but it would have winded him. The big man wasn't winded at all by the time they made it upstairs.

"First door on the left."

Brice followed Garrett into the master suite. It was a nice size, with a king-size bed and plenty of room to move around in. He directed Garrett to lay her on the bed.

"We've got to get your clothes off of you so we can bind your ribs." Brice began cutting the rest of her clothes off.

"Stop it. You're not going to, *ow!*" She grabbed Brice by the arm and squeezed.

"What's wrong?" he asked.

"I think it's my fault. I was pulling off her boots. I think her left ankle is broken. The boot didn't come off very easy. I'm sorry, ma'am." Garrett looked up with a pained expression.

"I'll check it next." Brice pulled the last piece of clothing from her top and reached around her to unfasten her bra.

"You're not taking that off. I mean it." Wild eyed, she glared at him then turned fearful eyes toward Garrett.

"We're not going to hurt you. I promise. You've got to have those ribs wrapped, and we can't do it without removing your bra. Look, I'm a paramedic. I'm used to doing this."

"Please," she whispered with tears in her eyes.

Brice saw the fear in her eyes and felt sorry for her, but knew it had to be done. She could puncture a lung if any of them were actually broken.

"I'm sorry. I've got to." He unhooked her bra and pulled it carefully off.

She had the prettiest, plumpest breasts he'd ever seen. He quickly masked his interest and had her sit up on the side of the bed with Garrett's help. He was careful to only touch her shoulders and arms.

"My foot is throbbing about as much as my head." The tears had started to leak from her eyes now in earnest.

"We'll take care of it next. Now I need you to put your arms on my shoulders while I wrap this around your ribs." He took the wrap and began at one side and wrapped it around her back. When he got to the front, there were two problems. They lay right where he needed to go with the wrap.

"Um, Garrett, I need you to hold her breasts up so I can get under them."

"Sure." He climbed on the bed behind her and reached around her to lift her breasts.

She began to sob now, and it was breaking his heart.

"Only one more time, and he can let them back down. He's not hurting you, is he?" Brice asked, knowing Garrett was being as careful not to be personal as possible.

"No," she whispered.

"Okay, you can let them down, Garrett." He finished wrapping her chest and taped it down. "It might be a little hard to breathe, but you should be able to. How does it feel?"

"Okay, I guess." She sniffed and didn't look at him.

"Let's look at the foot next." He helped her lie back down. Her foot was swollen but moved easily enough with some pain. "I don't think it's broken, but you're going to need something cold on it."

"I'll grab some wet cloths." Garrett disappeared into what was probably the master bath.

"Do you have something for pain I can get you?"

"Just some Tylenol. It's in the bathroom, too."

"I heard," Garrett called out.

"I've got to tend to the animals. I can't leave them without food and water."

"We'll take care of them for you. Don't worry about that right now." Brice took a cloth from Garrett when he reappeared. "Wrap those around her ankle."

"I'll go get some water next." Garrett handed the bottle of Tylenol to him.

Brice began wiping the blood from the lady's face with the wet cloth. It came away reluctantly, but her poor, abused face finally emerged. He winced at the bruising.

"I'm going to have to sew that cut up on your scalp."

"That's going to hurt, isn't it?" she asked.

"I'm afraid so. I'll be as quick as I can. Maybe it will only take a few stitches."

"What's your name?"

"I'm Brice, and my friend is Garrett. What about yours?"

"Ronnie. Um, thank you for helping me." She didn't look at him when she said it.

"No problem. What were you doing out?"

"Had to look for some more supplies."

Garrett returned with a glass of water and handed it to her. Brice held her up while she took the pain medicine. He eased her back down and searched in the first aid kit for the sutures.

"Ah, hell. You've got to sew her up?" Garrett winced.

"Yeah, that wound on her head will get infected if we don't close it. I'll need your help. You know why." They would probably have to hold her still.

"Yeah, I know." He eased onto the bed beside her and waited for Brice to get started.

"It shouldn't scar too bad, and it's under your hair, so you won't be able to see it."

"Just do it."

Brice made the first stick and she moaned. Garrett sat ready to grab her hands if she started to grab at Brice while he sewed. To her credit, she didn't, though she did cry and finally pass out.

"She did well, despite passing out," Garret said.

"She needs help, Garrett. She has animals that need to be taken care of. You up for it?"

"Sure, can't leave them untended."

"Her name is Ronnie."

"Pretty name," he said. "Will she be okay to leave her while we tend to things?"

"Yeah, throw the covers over her and let's get going. It's going to be dark soon."

"I don't like leaving her up here alone. What if she wakes up and tries to get up?"

Brice sighed. "She won't get far with that foot like it is. It's going to take both of us to get things done."

They stood looking at her for a few more seconds, then turned around and left her to rest.

Chapter Two

"She's a pretty little female," Garrett mused. "Not tiny, really, but strong looking."

"All that light brown hair will be pretty once she's gotten the blood out of it. It looks like honey." Brice grabbed a stool and a bucket and sat down to try his hand at milking a cow. Garrett's hands were too big.

Garrett busied himself with feeding and watering the horse and the other animals, which included the chickens. He put some feed in the coop, and they all followed him. He shut them up and hitched the latch.

She had the prettiest hazel eyes, with flecks of gold and green in them. She was all curvy, just like he liked a woman. He was a big man, and didn't like feeling like he would hurt a woman just by holding her in his arms. She had the most perfect, round ass he would love to explore. His cock had been hard ever since he'd held her. He wondered how Brice felt about her.

Ever since the year of catastrophes, when governments all over the world had collapsed, he and Brice had been a team. They'd been great friends since college but had grown even closer these last five years.

"I've gotten everything out here taken care of. How are you coming with milking?" Garrett asked.

"Well, the cow is a little pissed at me, but I've managed to get a half a bucket. I wonder how much she usually gets." Brice sighed and continued pulling on the teats with minimal luck.

Garrett chuckled. "I'm going to go deal with that deer. There should be some good meat to eat. I'll salvage what I can."

"I'll join you once I finish this."

Garrett walked out and started on the deer. It turned out to have quite a bit of useable meat. It had hit headfirst, so not much of the shoulder was affected. Brice emerged carrying the bucket of milk and took it into the kitchen. He returned a few seconds later and helped Garrett finish stripping the meat from the deer.

"I guess we're staying tonight," Garrett said.

"Yeah, she can't take care of herself like she is, much less this farm. Do you mind?"

"Nope. Don't mind a bit. She's a pretty lady."

"You getting interested in her?" Brice asked, looking up.

"I don't know. Maybe."

"We don't stick around in any one place for long. We have to keep scavenging to make a living."

"Yeah, I know." Garrett thought about settling down several times, but hadn't brought it up before.

"What are we going to do with the meat now?"

"Cook some of it for supper tonight." Garrett dropped the last piece of meat in the pan and stretched. "I'll get rid of the carcass while you take the meat in," Garrett said.

He dragged what was left of the deer deep into the woods and left it for the scavengers to have a feast. The smell shouldn't reach the house as far out as he left it. He returned to the house wanting to check on Ronnie. He liked the name. It even sounded strong.

He walked into the kitchen and noticed that Brice was putting the meat into the fridge. Despite there not being any electricity.

"Figure it would stay cooler in there."

"I'll cook some later. I want to go check on Ronnie."

"You're really stuck on her, aren't you?"

"I guess I am. I've haven't been around a female not in a brothel in over five years, Brice. It's nice for a change."

"I know what you mean." Brice nodded. "Go on up and let me know if I need to check on her."

Garrett all but ran up the stairs, but slowed down to peek in the bedroom before barging in. He didn't want to wake her up if she were sleeping. She had her head turned to the other side, so he couldn't tell if she was asleep or not. He eased into the bedroom and she turned her head with tear-filled eyes.

"Hey, don't cry. We've taken care of everything."

"What am I going to do? I can't work the farm like this. I'll lose everything and starve."

"I won't let you lose anything. I'll help you as long as you need the help." Garrett couldn't believe he'd just promised that.

"I can't ask you to do that." She still appeared to be uneasy around him. It bothered him.

"I'm not going to hurt you, Ronnie." It was important to him that she believed him.

She swallowed and nodded, but nothing changed in her demeanor.

"Is there anything I can get you right now?" he asked.

"No thanks. It's too soon for more Tylenol, so I'm just going to try to sleep some."

"I'm going to cook some of the deer meat for supper. I'll bring some to you when it's ready."

"I'm really not hungry." She picked at the cover with her good hand.

"We'll see how you feel later." Garrett backed out of the bedroom, leaving her to rest.

When he returned to the kitchen, it was to find Brice sitting down at the kitchen table sipping coffee he'd boiled on the stove.

"There's plenty more. I figure we'll need it to watch her. I'll have to wake her up every two hours to be sure she isn't suffering from an even worse concussion than I think she has."

Garrett put together a supper of deer meat, canned beans, and some bread that she obviously made from scratch. He was pleased to find that she had gas for cooking. They enjoyed the meal, and then Brice took some up to her so he could check her over. Garrett elected to stay downstairs and clean up the kitchen. He was afraid she would notice the state of his cock. It had only grown harder as the night wore on, because he couldn't get her out of his mind.

When Brice returned downstairs, he had a plate of half-eaten food. Garrett shook his head, but figured she didn't feel much like eating since she was still in a good amount of pain.

"Brice, I told her I would stick around until she was back on her feet. You don't have to stay if you don't want to. I know you don't like to stay in one place for long."

"I kind of promised the same thing," Brice confessed with a grin.

"Thanks. I just can't leave her like this."

"I guess I can't, either."

* * * *

Ronnie couldn't stop the tears from falling every little while. She'd worked so hard to remain independent and away from prying eyes. She knew if men ever found out about her being alone they would try and claim her, or worse, steal her for the black market. So far, she'd been able to avoid that.

Now, all her hard-won independence was threatened by two men. Two really big men. They had to each be six foot seven or so inches tall. Garrett had huge hands and was built like a tank. He had short black hair, with equally dark eyes. He scared her just by how big he was. Brice, on the other hand, was tall and lanky with a broad chest. His wasn't as defined as Garrett's seemed to be. He wasn't as large as Garret, either, just tall.

Brice had sandy blond hair that fell to his collar. His eyes were a bright, piercing blue the color of a robin's egg. They appeared to be great friends and worked well together. She wondered what they were doing in the area. Would they try and take her with them when they left? She would fight them. She didn't want to belong to any man, no matter how much her body reacted to them.

The entire time Brice had been in the room checking on her, her nipples had burned and stood at attention. She kept the covers tight around them to keep him from noticing. Her pussy wet her panties, and she worried he would smell her arousal. It wasn't right that these strangers should arouse her so much. She knew nothing about them. Besides, they would be moving on as soon as she managed to get back on her feet.

They wouldn't know how to put up the deer meat. She needed to be downstairs tending to it. She might make it to the stairs, but she would never make it down them. A fresh wave of tears fell at her predicament. It wasn't like her to cry at the drop of a hat. She was usually much stronger than this.

She heard the sounds of boots on the stairs. Garrett stuck his head around the corner of the door and grinned to find her awake.

"How are you feeling?" he asked, walking further into the room.

"My head hurts, and my wrist and ankle throb. I'm crying and can't quit, and the deer needs processing and salting."

"I was wondering how you preserved it. Tell me what to do, and I'll try to handle it for you."

"You've already done so much. I can't ask you to do more work. It will be dark soon, and I know you will want to get back to wherever you were going."

"I told you, I'm sticking around until you're able to handle things on your own again. So tell me what to do about the deer meat."

She swallowed and instructed him on salting and preserving the meat. "I have a cellar that stays cool. I hang the meat in there once I've finished with it."

"I'll take care of it before we come up to bed tonight." Garrett smiled at her before turning and heading back downstairs.

* * * *

Several hours later, he finished the process and needed to clean up. The house had begun to cool down pretty rapidly now. They would have to sleep with Ronnie to keep her warm. Brice had said that with broken ribs she would be susceptible to pneumonia, and that would be dangerous without antibiotics to give her. She wasn't going to like them sleeping with her, he was sure, he thought with a grin.

"Brice, I'm going to head upstairs and take a shower."

"I'll take one after you, and then we better get to bed. I have a feeling there's more to do tomorrow. Plus, I'll have to milk that stupid cow again."

Garrett chuckled and took the stairs two at a time. He was eager to find out what she felt like up close, without clothes in the way. He carried his bag of things into the bathroom with him and noticed Ronnie was sleeping.

The water proved to be lukewarm at best, but helped to curb his raging dick from raring to go to mildly interested. No doubt that would change once he climbed into bed with her. He wondered how Brice was faring. Did his friend not feel anything for her? It would be the first time they had not felt the same intense arousal for the same woman. They'd shared women since back in college nearly ten years ago.

Once he was out of the shower and drying off, Brice walked in with his bag.

"She's going to be pissed when we climb into bed with her," Brice said.

"I know. Guard your nuts."

Brice chuckled. "Don't worry."

"Should I hold off till you get out? Might make it easier if we double-team her."

"Not a bad idea. I'll hurry."

Garrett walked into the bedroom in nothing but his thermal pants. He didn't worry with the shirt. She didn't rouse at all. He sat on the edge of the bed on her right side. He didn't want to sleep on her left side with her ribs. Brice would be careful of them.

Twenty minutes later, Brice walked out in his thermals. It was obvious that his friend *was* affected by Ronnie. Brice's thermals were tented just like his. They climbed into bed on either side of her. Ronnie roused with wide eyes.

"What are you doing?"

"Going to bed," Brice pointed out.

"In bed with me?"

"We'll all stay warm better this way," Garrett said.

"As long as you realize nothing is going to happen." She seemed fine with sharing the bed.

"We aren't going to hurt you," Brice promised her.

"You're fucking hard!" she all but yelled.

"Doesn't mean anything." Brice pulled the cover up higher and turned away from her, but scooted closer to her.

"Men can't handle hard-ons without fucking someone. Are you going to fuck each other, then?"

"Not hardly, but we don't have to have sex just because we got hard." Garrett couldn't believe they were having this conversation. Maybe he could.

He curled up around her. "Go to sleep, Ronnie. I promise, we won't do anything but sleep."

She was stiff and unyielding for several minutes before she finally relaxed and fell asleep. Holding her felt so good. It felt right. It worried him that he felt that way. He wondered how Brice was feeling. He didn't dare ask, for fear of waking Ronnie back up. She needed to rest. It would go a long way to helping her heal.

He worried she would develop pneumonia as Brice had warned. Garrett decided he didn't need to borrow trouble. They already had plenty of that. He closed his eyes and drifted off to sleep.

* * * *

Brice lay awake for a long time. His dick was hard and throbbing. He couldn't believe he was reacting to her like this. Sure, she was good-looking, and so much like what he and Garrett liked in a woman, but it was obvious she wanted to remain independent. Plus, they were scavengers and moved around a lot. It was how they made their living. They'd never even considered putting down roots.

He thought about milking the cow and nearly laughed aloud at his poor attempts. He'd never believed he would even try such a thing. He wasn't the domestic type. He could admit the house was nice. If he were going to settle down, he would want something just like this, big and open and airy.

He couldn't help but hope Ronnie would warm up to them and maybe let them love her while they were there. It had been a long time for them, and they didn't like frequenting the brothels because the women had been sold on the black market. When they had, he and Garrett treated them really well. They never hurt them and made sure they were pleasured as well. Still, they always felt guilty and hadn't been near one in over six months.

Brice had come by his own hand more in the last six months than he had in over six years. It was a temporary solution, but was hardly satisfying. He was sure Garrett felt the same way.

How long had Ronnie been out here on her own? As well as the farm seemed to be doing, it had to have been a while. He wondered if she lost all her family and friends in the hell that had fallen on the earth. He and Garrett had lost their entire family and their friends as well. Garrett had been serious about a woman, and she died in the plagues that followed the catastrophes. For a long time, he hadn't spoken much. It was only in the last two years that he'd even been interested in sex.

Brice hoped that his being interested in Ronnie was a good sign, though how she would take their interest was anybody's guess. Somehow they had to soften her up toward them. They would be there with her for a few weeks, with her in such bad shape. He still wasn't sure if her wrist and ankle were broken or not. Without an X-ray, there was no way to tell.

He guessed they were going to learn some lessons on farm life over the next few weeks. It would be good practice for when they did settle down in one place. Right now, though, they were content traveling around gathering goods that people needed and trading them for food and gas. That was about all they needed in their life.

Well, maybe that was all they needed. Right now, he was wondering if they needed a certain feisty little female named Ronnie.

Chapter Three

Brice had set a mechanical alarm clock and woke her up every two hours. He wanted to be sure she was lucid and not suffering any further problems. She wasn't at all happy when he did. Each time she woke up, Garrett woke, too. Around seven, Brice got up and dressed to start the day. It would be a long one, he was sure. He had never really worked on a farm, so this would be a true adventure for him. Well, he planned to look at it as an adventure.

Garrett made it down about the time he poured up the coffee. The big man looked a little worse for wear. He imagined he didn't look much better, considering the lack of sleep they'd both suffered.

"Morning, Garrett."

"Morning. How do you think she's doing?"

"I think she's fine as far as her head goes. Her wrist and ankle both look better. I'm leaning toward their being badly sprained, and not broken."

"What about her ribs?" Garrett pulled out some deer meat that he'd cooked the night before and began making breakfast for them.

"I don't have any way of knowing that. All we can do is hope for the best." Brice took a sip of the bitter coffee.

"What are the plans for the day?" Garrett asked.

"Well, first off is milking that dang cow and gathering eggs. I'll do that part. You might want to check with her on what else needs doing. I've never really been on a farm before."

"Well, I've done a lot of hunting and been on horses some, but I'm not going to be much help, either. Let's just hope there isn't a lot to it." Garrett served up breakfast.

As soon as they finished eating, Garrett cleaned up and they walked outside to figure out what was first. By the sound of the chickens and the cow, they were late.

"I'll check on feeding the cows and the horse," Garrett said.

Brice carried the bucket into the barn and noticed the cow was moving restlessly in her stall. "Sorry I'm late. Had a rough night."

Shaking his head, he sat down to start the torturous process of squeezing milk from an ornery cow. After a good twenty minutes, he'd gotten about the same amount of milk as the night before, so he stopped and carried the milk to the house to come back out with a basket to gather the eggs.

The minute he opened the chicken coop, he was attacked by what felt like a hundred mad birds. In actuality, he realized later, there had only been about twelve. He scooped up the eggs and returned to the kitchen without having seen or heard from Garrett in all that time. He wondered what his friend had found to keep him busy.

He cleaned up in the laundry room sink before climbing the stairs to see about Ronnie. He hoped she would be in better spirits after resting more. They had been gone a good three hours.

He found her sitting up on the side of the bed, shaking all over.

"What in the hell are you doing up?"

"I need to go to the bathroom. I can't walk, and I was going to try to crawl, but my side hurts too much to bend over." There were tears in her eyes.

"Aw, damn, baby. Let me help you. Then we'll get some clothes for you." Brice scooped her into his arms and carried her to the bathroom.

He stood her on her good leg in front of the toilet and left her there to look for something for her to put on. He searched through the drawers and found little to nothing for clothing. He finally located a couple of pairs of jeans and work shirts, along with the bare minimum of underwear. Why didn't she have more clothes?

He decided the best thing was to take her downstairs and sit her on the couch in front of the fireplace to keep her warm. He confiscated one of Garrett's large shirts, since it would be bigger than his. It would cover her from neck to knees. He heard the toilet flush, so returned and knocked on the door.

"You ready in there?"

"Just about. Give me a minute."

Brice heard the sink turn on then off. He figured she was washing her face and hands. She needed a shower, but he would need Garrett's help with that. It would take one of them to hold her up and the other to bathe her. She would be fine until later that afternoon.

"Okay, I'm ready."

He opened the door to find her leaning against the counter with a towel wrapped around her. Her face had gone pale and she was plumb white around her lips. She was in a lot of pain. Brice picked her up and carried her back to the bed, where he carefully sat her back down.

"I've got underwear for you to put on and a big shirt to cover you. You can't wear jeans with your ankle like it is. We'd have a hell of a time getting them on and off."

She fingered the large shirt. "Whose is it? It's not one of mine."

"No, it's Garrett's. His are big enough to cover you to your knees. I'm going to carry you downstairs so you can sit on the couch, where you'll be warm enough with the fire."

"Um, can I have some more Tylenol?"

"Sure you can. I'll get that for you once we get you dressed." Brice started pulling the towel off.

"No! I mean, I can do it. You just wait for me outside."

"You can't do it by yourself. You can't bend, and you can't use your wrist to button up the shirt," he pointed out.

Defeat drifted over her face, and she just nodded and dropped the towel as if it really didn't matter anymore. That gesture alone broke his heart. He quickly put the shirt on her and buttoned it up in record time. Then he helped her stand so he could pull down her underwear.

Once she had them off, he had her sit back down so he could slide the fresh pair up her legs. Then she stood up again and he finished pulling them up.

"There. That's over with. It will get better from here, Ronnie. I promise."

She didn't say anything, just nodded and sighed. Dressing had worn her out. He gently picked her up and carried her downstairs to the couch. He didn't do half-bad, he decided, but then, he'd been going downstairs. Garrett would need to carry her back up. He just wasn't as strong as the big guy.

"Let me get you some Tylenol and something to drink. Then I'll start a fire in the fireplace."

"Hey, I'll do that." Garrett walked into the room.

"Great. Thanks."

He heard Garrett talking to Ronnie as he ran back upstairs to get the painkiller and back to the kitchen for water. By the time he had returned, Garrett was laying wood for a fire.

"Here you go, Ronnie." He handed her the pills and water.

"Thanks, both of you, for helping me. I know I'm hard to get along with, but I've been on my own for a long time. I'm not used to being around people, especially men." She swallowed the pills with the water.

"No problem. We need to sit down and find out exactly what all needs doing so we don't miss anything." Garrett had the fire started and was fanning the flames.

"I'm going to go heat up some water. I want you to soak your wrist and ankle in some warm water. It will help get the swelling down." Brice winked and left Garrett alone with her.

* * * *

Garrett stood up after getting the fire started and busied himself arranging the covers over her.

Ronnie could tell he was nervous about being around her. To tell the truth, she was nervous about being alone with him. He was so big. Big men tended to be mean. So far, he hadn't been anything but nice to her. Still, you never knew.

"We've milked the cow, gotten in the eggs, fed the horse and cow in the barn, and I threw hay out for the cows in your pasture. I found a garden that looks like you have something planted, but I didn't know what it was."

"It's turnip and mustard greens. They're cold-weather vegetables. Already got everything else in for the winter." She stared into the fire, thinking maybe he would leave now.

He sat down on the corner of the couch. "So is there anything more that needs doing?"

"Always something needs doing around a place this size. I work on things as I get time. I've been looking for a smaller place that's in good shape. This one is too big for just me, but it was all I could find when I needed a place."

"How long you been on your own?"

"'Bout three years." She couldn't believe she was telling him all of this.

Hell, she couldn't believe how her body was reacting around him. Her breasts were heavy and her nipples peaked. She had already wet her panties with her pussy juices. At this rate, they would know she was interested in them and want to have sex. She didn't want to have it ever again.

"Why are you by yourself? Don't you know how dangerous it is for a female alone? There are black market agents out there looking for women they can steal." Garrett looked worried for her sake.

"I'm careful. I don't go out much. Just when I have to get supplies, and I don't go to Barter Town at all."

"How do you find enough to live off of?"

"I manage." She held up her head, daring him to say she wasn't managing just fine.

"You've done a lot, that's for sure."

"I'm a hard worker."

"Where were you before you moved here?" he asked.

"Nowhere good." She leaned back against the pillow on the couch and shut her eyes, hoping to stop the inquisition.

Instead, he pushed on, as if eager to know everything about her.

"Brice and I have known each other since college and have been working together ever since the year of catastrophes. We mostly salvage and trade for what we need. Haven't thought about settling down yet. Maybe someday, though."

"So you've been salvaging for the last five years?" She opened her eyes to find him staring at her with a puzzled look in his eyes.

"Yep." He smiled at her.

She couldn't help herself. She smiled back. Maybe he wasn't so bad after all. Then she looked down at his lap and notice his cock was standing straight up. She shivered and backed farther into the couch. He caught her looking at him and cursed.

"Ronnie, I can't help it. You're a beautiful woman. I'm not going to jump on you, though. You're safe. I would never force a woman." He looked desperate for her to believe him.

She couldn't help her reaction. Sex meant pain, and she didn't want to remember the pain.

"Please, just go for now."

"I'm sorry, Ronnie." He hung his head and walked into the kitchen.

Ronnie felt like a heel for hurting his feelings, but he scared her like that. Either of them could easily take advantage of her like she was. What was she going to do? She needed them to keep her farm going and she was alienating them left and right. She needed to get control of her fear.

It had been so long since she'd been around a man, much less two of them as large as they were, that she wasn't sure how to act normally. All she could think about was the last time she'd dealt with one.

Right after the flood that had ripped through her town in Arkansas, Ronnie found herself alone and scared of what to do. She'd survived where most of the people in the town had not, including her family and most of her friends. When Carl offered to take care of her, she'd jumped at the chance. She'd known him most of her life but hadn't been around him that much. He was a couple of years older than her.

At first, it had been okay. He'd made sure she had clothes and food, and she kept house for him. Then he started pressuring her into having sex with him. He'd said that since the world was in such a mess that men and women just hooked up and became common-law husbands and wives. She'd finally given in, and that was when the abuse had started.

She shook herself, refusing to let it get the best of her now. She was stronger now. She could choose not to think about it. She hadn't had a nightmare in nearly a year now. Hopefully she wouldn't have one with these men there with her.

Brice walked in carrying a bucket of water and placed it on the floor near her swollen ankle.

"It's pretty warm, so you might want to test it with your heel to be sure it's not too hot for you. I found some Epsom salts, so I added that."

Ronnie lowered her heel into the water and decided it was just right. She submerged her foot into the water and hummed her appreciation. It felt wonderful.

"Thanks, it feels great."

"Okay, be right back with the one for your wrist." Seconds later, he returned with another smaller bucket he placed on the couch next to her.

"Try it now and be sure it's not too hot." He watched her test it with her fingers then let her hand sink below the water.

She lifted her head to tell him thanks and found her face next to his. She could smell him. He smelled woodsy with just a hint of male sweat. It was like an aphrodisiac to her. She leaned toward him, then caught herself and pulled back, concentrating on her hand to cover her lapse of judgment.

If he had noticed, he didn't say anything. Instead, he stirred the fire and added a log. Then he sat down in a chair close to the couch and watched her with a strange look on his face.

"What?" she finally asked, unable to stand his scrutiny any longer.

"Just wondering how you've managed to take care of yourself so well all alone. You're a remarkable woman."

"I've had to, so I did it. You can do anything if you have to. It was either survive or die. I chose to survive."

"And you've done it very well. I admire you."

"You do?" She was confused now.

"Yes. It takes a strong person to live out here in the Border Lands. A lot of men don't make it."

"Are you going to turn me over to a black market agent?"

Chapter Four

"No! We would never do that to you. Why would you think such a thing?" Brice jumped from his chair.

"Because you're scavengers and sell and trade things. I would bring you a lot of gas or food."

"None of that is worth your life. I know what sort of life you would have if they sold you to a brothel or some man who wouldn't treat you well. There's no way we'd ever do that to you. Get that out of your head right now."

"How do you expect me to believe you? I don't know you at all."

"Trust me. There's no way either of us would ever do anything to hurt you." Brice shook his head and walked into the kitchen, where Garrett stood by the stove, fixing lunch.

"I guess you heard all of that," Brice said.

"Yeah, I freaked her out because I'm hard and she saw it. I can't control my fucking dick around her." Garrett banged a pot down as he added something to the pan he was stirring.

"There has to be a way to win her trust." Brice paced the kitchen.

"She's never going to welcome us in her bed. We might as well get that off our minds," Garrett added.

"She needs loving more than any woman I've ever known. She's been abused. You can tell by the fear she has in her eyes when we're close to her."

"Yeah, I figured that, too."

"It will just take time, and right now, we have plenty of that. She isn't going to be on her feet anytime soon. You up to hanging around for a few weeks?"

"Fine by me. I like the area, and am enjoying doing the chores. Of course I'm not stuck with the cow and the egg collecting like you are," he pointed out with a grin.

Brice made as if to throw a cup at him. "You're stuck with kitchen duty, though."

"I can handle it. Speaking of which, I'm going to let you carry her plate to her." He spooned up deer steak and gravy with biscuits.

Brice lifted an eyebrow at Garrett cutting up her meat.

"She only has one hand."

"I'll try to get her to eat a little more. She seems livelier than she was last night." Brice took the plate and returned to the living room.

"How's the water?"

"Getting cooler now."

"I've brought you some lunch. You need to eat so you'll heal faster. I know you want us out of your hair." She took the plate one-handed.

Brice took a towel and dried off her hand, then removed the bucket. Then he did the same thing with her foot.

"They both already look better. We'll do it again tonight before bed."

"Did you cut up my meat for me?" she asked.

"No, Garrett did it. He figured you couldn't do it one-handed."

"Um, tell him I said thanks." She looked down at her plate and began eating.

Brice returned and ate with Garrett in the kitchen.

"She said thanks for cutting up her meat for her. I honestly wouldn't have thought of that."

"Just figured she only had one hand." Garrett gathered their dishes and put them in the sink to wash later.

"I think I could take a nap before it's time to work on the evening chores," Garrett said.

"Doesn't sound like a bad idea to me."

They walked into the living room to choose chairs to relax in. Brice noticed Ronnie had nearly cleaned her plate and set it on one side of the couch. He picked it up and carried it back to the kitchen. Then he helped her arrange herself on the couch for a nap.

"We've got a few hours, so we thought a little down time would do us all good, considering how little sleep we got last night." Garrett settled himself in a recliner and got comfortable.

He noticed Garrett had chosen another one and was already reared back and looked to be already asleep. He'd know for sure when he started snoring. The big guy snored low, but enough you noticed it. He always teased him about it. He wondered what Ronnie would think.

Finally he settled down, and though his mind kept churning wondering about her background, he finally fell asleep.

* * * *

Ronnie woke up sweating. She felt like something was sitting on her chest. She coughed and coughed, and immediately, Brice was by her side.

"Damn, you're getting sick. We've got to get you back to bed and bundled up.'"

"Why am I getting sick? I don't get sick." She began coughing again.

Garrett jumped up and walked over. "What's going on? Why is she coughing?"

"She's getting sick. Carry her upstairs and get her in the bed just like she is. Cover her with all the covers you can find." He felt of her forehead. "She's got a fever. We need to sweat it out of her."

Garrett gently picked her up and carried her upstairs while Brice grabbed the medicine. He walked into the room with a glass of water and gave her two Tylenol while Garrett held her up.

"I'm going to go fight that cow and put up the chickens. You get in bed with her and keep her warm until I get back. Then you can do whatever chores you have next."

"Really, I'll be okay in a little while. You don't have to get in bed with me." She hated that her voice wobbled.

Garrett had already pulled off his boots and was taking off his shirt then his jeans. He had on thermals, which didn't do much to ease her mind. Especially considering his dick was tenting them. She immediately snapped her eyes back up to him. He looked miserable.

She turned over on her left side and winced, but once she settled, it actually felt better, especially when she coughed. The bed dipped and he climbed beneath the covers. Then he spooned her from behind. He wrapped an arm around her waist. His cock was caught between them in the small of her back. She could feel his hot breath on the back of her neck.

To his credit, he didn't try anything. He just held her close. She wanted to turn over and find out what his kiss would be like but decided that was just the fever talking. She knew better. Kissing led to other things, and she was not going there.

"Relax and try to rest. Are you having trouble breathing? You're panting."

"It's a little hard to take a deep breath, and it makes me cough."

"Coughing is probably a good thing to get all that stuff out of your lungs."

"But it hurts, Garrett." She sniffed.

"It's okay, baby. Just snuggle up to me and I'll keep you warm. If you need to cough, let me know, and I'll hold your ribs for you." Garrett's voice sounded so sincere.

"Thanks," she whispered.

The more she breathed, the harder it became, and when she coughed, it hurt so bad. Then she began to shiver all over. Garrett all but lay on top of her, trying to keep her warm.

She heard Brice walk into the room. He took one look at the situation and cursed.

"It hasn't been four hours yet, so I can't give you any more Tylenol. Let's add another comforter. I'll go grab one off another bed."

He disappeared out the bedroom door but returned seconds later with another comforter. He settled it over her, then stripped down to his thermals and climbed into the bed with her.

"Do I need to go do anything?" Garrett asked.

"I fed the horses and the cow and the chickens. There was still hay out in the pasture, so I think they are all right for the night."

"I-I can't stop sh-shaking," she told them.

"I know. We'll get you warm soon." Brice eased closer to her.

She no longer cared that they were in the bed with her. She was miserable. Between her chest hurting and not being able to take deep breaths, not to mention the shakes, Ronnie welcomed them there.

She drifted toward sleep, but instead of sleeping, she began to hallucinate instead. She remembered Carl forcing himself on her and telling her it was only fair. He was taking care of her. She'd tried to endure it and ended up fighting him. He hit her, and that had been the beginning of the abuse.

The pain was terrible when he hurt her. She'd try to make sure everything was perfect for him, but it was never enough to suit him. She tossed and turned in the bed, crying out from her ribs and ankle. She knew someone was trying to soothe her, but Carl was always there with his fists.

Sometime after midnight, her fever broke and she sweated something fierce. She was dimly aware of someone stripping her and bathing her and re-dressing her. They'd changed the sheets as well. It felt so good to lie back on the cool, crisp sheets. Finally, she rested and never noticed that the men held her through the night.

The next morning, she woke up feeling much better. She still had a cough, but it was productive, and she no longer had a fever. She needed to go to the bathroom and was covered up by two very large men. She wasn't sure who to wake up. Finally, she chose Garrett because he was closer to the bathroom.

"Garrett?" she whispered.

He instantly woke and stared at her. "Is something wrong? Do you need me to wake Brice?"

"No, I need to go to the bathroom. Can you carry me?" She wouldn't look him in the eyes. It was embarrassing to have to ask.

"Of course, baby. Hold on and let me get up." He climbed out of bed, then reached over and picked her up with no effort at all. She felt safe that he wouldn't drop her while she was in his arms.

He carried her to the bathroom and left her standing by the counter with a firm word to call him when she was finished. He made her promise, which she thought was cute.

She finished and washed her hands, then looked in the mirror and realized they'd actually bathed her. Even her hair, for the most part, was clean of blood. She still had some around the stitches. She felt clean, and it felt good. They'd really taken care of her. It made her feel bad about the way she'd treated them. But she had no idea what kind of men they actually were. Maybe she could begin to trust that they were decent men after all.

She called out that she was ready, and Garrett opened the door and walked in the bathroom to pick her up. He carried her back to bed and tucked the sheets around her and Brice.

"Where are you going?" she asked.

"It's morning. Time to do chores. I'm going to fix coffee and breakfast. Brice should wake up in a little bit. He'll be glad to know you're feeling so much better."

"Thanks, Garrett, for taking care of me. I appreciate it."

"It's my pleasure, Ronnie. I want you well again."

He walked out of the room and she heard him walking down the stairs. He wanted her well again. Did that mean he was ready to move on again? For some reason, that made her sad. She'd gotten used to them being there. Surely they wouldn't leave before she was completely healed.

A few minutes later, the aroma of coffee reached the room, and Brice stirred. He finally lifted his head and sniffed. One eye opened then the other. She giggled.

"Hey, you're feeling better," he observed.

"I do feel much better. I just wish my side didn't hurt so much when I cough."

"That will take time. Give it a chance." He rolled out of bed, then tucked the covers around her. "Do you need to go to the bathroom before I go downstairs?"

"Um, thanks, but Garrett took me. I had to wake him up."

"Okay, we'll bring you something up to eat before we head out for chores." He began to pull on jeans and his shirt, then his boots. "Keep the covers over you, even if you feel warm enough."

"Okay. I will. I don't want to get sick again. It was terrible."

"Won't be long before you'll be on your feet again. You'll see."

She watched him walk out, then heard his tread on the stairs. It sounded like they were both looking forward to her recovery. It hurt to think they wanted to leave. She would never have believed she would be sad about them leaving.

* * * *

"Did you hear her talking in her delirium?" Garrett asked Brice.

"Yeah. She's had it rough. Some bastard named Carl abused her. I wish I could teach him a thing or two about how to treat a woman."

"Me too."

Garrett couldn't imagine someone wanting to hurt her. She was so beautiful and sweet. Sure, she was rough around the edges at first, but she'd warmed up to them quickly enough. With time, he was sure they could win her over. He just wasn't sure how much time they had left. Brice said a few weeks, but was that enough time to change her mind about men?

"What's for breakfast?" Brice asked, breaking into his musings.

"Omelets. We have plenty of eggs that will spoil if we don't do something with them."

"Sounds good. You know, she could trade her eggs and milk if she didn't have to worry about being grabbed." Brice seemed to think about it.

"If she had a man with her, no one would bother her," Garrett added.

Brice sipped his coffee.

Garrett could tell his buddy was thinking about it. Maybe he was thinking about settling down. He sure hoped so. He'd been thinking a good bit about it lately. He wouldn't mind settling down with Ronnie. They just had to convince her.

"You're thinking awfully hard over there, Garrett." Brice sipped his coffee.

"Ever thought about settling down?" Garrett finally broached the subject.

"Not until now. You thinking about settling down here?"

"Yeah, the idea has crossed my mind."

"How are you going to talk Ronnie into letting you?"

"I was sort of hoping you might want to settle down here, too." Garrett watched his friend closely.

"I guess. I haven't let myself think along those lines because she's so leery of us."

"I want to try to convince her. I think she's closer to accepting us now. She just needs to know we aren't going to force her into anything." Garrett walked over to the doorway and looked in on Ronnie.

"She is going to get caught if she continues to go out looking for supplies by herself. I can't stand the idea of some black market agent grabbing her," Garrett continued.

"If she won't accept us, there's nothing we can do about it."

"I know. Doesn't make it any easier to take."

Garrett finished making Brice's omelet and slid it on a plate for him. Then he made another one and took it into the living room to Ronnie.

"Hope you like omelets," he said.

"Love them. I eat a lot of them with all the eggs I end up with."

He watched her dig into the food and enjoyed watching her eat. She looked up and smiled once, then returned to her meal. When she had finished, he leaned in to take her plate, and she surprised him by kissing him quickly on the cheek.

"Thanks for breakfast, Garrett."

"No problem."

He left her in the living room smiling so big that Brice asked what was wrong with him. He just shook his head and smiled wider. He didn't want to share that just yet. He'd keep that to himself for now. She was warming up to them. Maybe if she did, by the time she was able to handle the farm by herself, Brice would have decided to stick around. He sure intended to.

Chapter Five

Ronnie felt much better after four days on the couch doing nothing but lounging like a kept woman. She quickly changed her thoughts from that. She was still injured and wasn't really attractive to them right now. They'd probably start trying to push themselves on her once she healed.

Still, they'd been so kind to her. They'd kept her farm going and treated her like a princess. She smiled to herself. She hadn't thought about princesses in a very long time. She could remember growing up believing in them. She'd been convinced her prince would sweep her away one day. Instead, she'd ended up with an ogre.

She stretched and picked her foot up off the pillow on the couch and looked at her still slightly swollen ankle. It was a mirage of colors. She could wiggle her toes much easier now, and even move her ankle without too much pain. Her wrist wasn't a lot better. It hurt to move it and was swollen all the way down her hand. Still, she could wiggle her fingers.

Maybe they wanted to settle down with her because she had a farm already established. Maybe she wasn't even the reason they were sticking around to help her. Still, they seemed to keep swollen cocks around her. They assured her they were fine and wouldn't force themselves on her. But maybe she was beginning to want them.

The idea of kissing them had grown in her head for several days now. She often stared at their lips when they were asleep, wondering if she could brush them and not wake them up. She was too chicken to try it. She stayed wet around them, and her breasts would grow heavy. Several times when they were out tending to the farm, she'd been tempted to masturbate but was afraid they would come in and catch her.

Did they jack off? She would like to watch them do that. For some reason it sounded so intimate and sensual. *Ronnie, you're getting in over your head here. Have you forgotten what sex is really like?*

She heard the back door open and close. A draft of cold air blew into the living room and hit her. She shivered and looked over at the fire. It was close to going out. She hoped one of them would come in and check on her.

It turned out to be Brice. He walked in and smiled at her.

"How are you doing?"

"I'm fine. Um, can you put another log on the fire?" She smiled sheepishly.

"No problem." He added the log and stirred the embers.

"It seems like I'm always asking you for something. I'm sorry. I don't mean to be demanding. You're already doing so much for me."

"You're not demanding. Get that out of your head. We like doing things for you." He did something he'd never done before. He leaned in and kissed her forehead. "How about something to drink?"

"That would be great. Tea, if there's any left."

"Garrett made some fresh last night. I'll get you a glass and we can talk for a while."

He walked into the kitchen but returned a few seconds later with two glasses of tea. He handed her one and took his over to the lounge chair to sit down.

"What did you want to talk about?" she asked cautiously.

Was he going to tell her they would be leaving soon? She was going to be on her feet before too much longer. Maybe he was going to suggest they become intimate, and she wasn't sure she was ready for that.

"About what you're going to do about staying alone. I'm worried about you."

"I'm okay. I've been on my own for three years now. I'll be fine."

"More and more people are coming to the Border Lands to escape the violence in the communities back there. Some of them are good people, but some of them aren't so nice. With more people out here, it's going to be harder for you to stay hidden."

"What do you think I should do?" She was scared of what he would say.

"You really do need to find a good man to take care of you. Someone you trust, of course."

"Trust isn't easy for me." She sipped her tea and looked at the fire.

"We know some of what you went through. You talked while you were sick. Not all men are like this Carl person, Ronnie."

"How am I supposed to know the difference? It could be too late by the time I find out he's not trustworthy."

"We could look for one for you that we trust," Brice suggested quietly.

"I-I don't know."

"Do you trust us, Ronnie?"

There it was. The question she'd been anticipating for days now. How to answer it? She wanted to tell them the truth, but she didn't want to pressure them into staying when they obviously were ready to go.

"Yes, I trust you. You've been nothing but kind to me, and worked hard for me. How could I not trust you?"

"So you would feel comfortable with someone we picked out?" he asked.

"I don't know. I'm comfortable around you and Garrett now. But you've been nothing but gentleman. Of course, I'm not really in any shape for, um. Anyway. I'll be better off by myself. Maybe I'll move farther west."

Brice stood up and crossed to the couch. He sat on the edge of it. "I'd hate for you to give up this place. It's a really nice place, and you've already done so much work to it."

Ronnie swallowed around the lump that had grown in her throat when he moved closer. She felt the now-familiar wetness between her legs.

"I do like it here. But I've had some close calls recently, so it's probably time to think about moving." She looked down at the as yet untouched glass of tea she was holding.

"You've had someone bothering you? Here at the house?"

"Once I had someone come up to the house and demand to see my man. I told him he wasn't there, to come back later. He never showed back up. I kept the gun on him the entire time. Then there have been the times I've nearly been caught out scavenging." She took a tentative sip of her tea to see if it would go down around the lump in her throat.

"See, that is why you need a man to help you and take care of you."

She started to tell him that she had been doing fine without one for the last three years, but he stopped her.

"I know you've been taking care of yourself, but a man can keep other men away from you and protect you so that you don't have to worry as much about them bothering you. He can help around the farm, too. You have a lot on you here. It's taking me and Garrett to keep up with the place."

"I'm sorry you've had so much to do."

"I'm not complaining about it. Just making a statement. You could use help, Ronnie."

"I'll think about it. Do you already know someone you're thinking about?" She hoped not. If she allowed anyone into her life, it would be one of them.

"I know a few men, but I'd have to think about it. I know you need someone sensitive to your, um, history." Brice looked down at his nearly empty tea glass and turned it up to gulp down the rest.

"I better get back out there and finish up the chores I'm working on. Garrett is a slave driver," he said with a grin.

"Thanks for the tea. I was thirsty." She took another sip and sat it on the end table next to her.

"One of us will be back in to check on you in a little while."

She watched Brice walk back through the kitchen until he was out of sight. She liked watching both men walk away from her, because they had such delectable asses. She sighed and pondered her predicament.

There had actually been a couple of occasions when men had come to the house and tried to get in. She'd scared them off with the gun, but she knew one day one would catch her outside unawares if she wasn't careful. Then there had been the close calls while she'd been out scavenging. One man had gotten so close as to have her in his hands, but she'd managed to fight her way clear. Her time was running out and she knew it. Why wouldn't they just leave her alone? She wasn't anything to look at. She was heavy for a female, and awkward.

Sighing, she leaned back against the back of the couch. What if she could convince one of the men to stay? The other one could come visit any time he wanted to. Who would she ask? She thought long and hard, and realized she couldn't choose. She liked both of them, and her body reacted to both of them.

Garrett's extra-large body didn't really frighten her anymore, and Brice seemed to have a good head on his shoulders. Garrett remembered to be careful of her injuries and tried hard to make her smile. Brice tended to her and made sure she was comfortable. Both men were wonderful, for men. Still, they were men, and all men wanted sex. The bad thing was, she was beginning to be interested in sex as well. Mostly she was interested in sex with them.

* * * *

Brice and Garrett took a breather from fixing the fence they'd found down in the pasture. Despite the chill in the air, they were sweating.

"So, what did she say when you offered to find a man for her?" Garrett asked.

He really didn't like the idea of looking for a man for her. For some reason it bothered him to think of her with another man. He realized he had become very protective of her and thought of her as his to take care of.

"She wasn't real excited about it. She said she would think about it, but I don't think she's going to go for the idea."

"She's not safe here anymore. More and more people are moving out this direction."

"She admitted she'd had some close calls already, but she seems to think she's better off by herself than with a man she doesn't know." Brice wiped the sweat off his forehead with the back of his sleeve.

"Maybe we should stay with her, Brice. I mean I know we haven't thought about settling down before now, but what would it hurt? It's a nice place. She's a nice woman." Garrett leaned against the fence without looking at him.

"I don't know. I really hadn't planned to settle down just yet. I mean, we're not that old. We could still pick a nice place later."

"More people moving out this way, we may have to go farther west by then to find a place." Garrett looked up at Brice.

"Not a lot of places left out west of here. The earthquake took out most everything around California, and the drought got most of the rest." Brice shook his head and picked up the hammer and nails. "Let's keep looking for another few minutes before we turn around and go back."

Garrett nodded and grabbed the bundle of wire in his gloved hands. Maybe if Brice didn't want to settle down, he would. Only she wasn't as comfortable around him as she was around Brice. She'd accept him with Brice, but he wasn't so sure she would if it were just him. It bothered him that she was still uneasy around him.

They walked another twenty minutes without finding any more broken areas in the fence line. Brice called a halt to it and they turned around and headed back to the house. Garrett walked on ahead, eager to get back and see Ronnie. He hoped she was feeling better today. Her wrist still seemed swollen. Brice had said he was worried it had a broken bone in it, but there was nothing he could do other than soak it and wrap it.

As soon as they arrived back at the house, Garrett hurried and put up the wire and hammer he had so he could go check on Ronnie. Brice seemed to realize what he was doing, because he took his time putting up his hammer and nails. Garrett wasn't waiting on him. He hurried toward the back door and only stopped in the laundry room to remove his dirty boots, jacket, and hat.

He found her napping on the couch with her feet up and her left hand over the back of the couch. She had told him it didn't hurt as bad when she had it up. He didn't want to wake her up, but he dearly wanted to talk with her. He loved listening to her slight Southern accent. He and Brice were originally from the Chicago area, so they were fascinated by her accent.

He turned to leave her alone, but she stirred and opened her eyes. At first, she looked startled, but then her eyes softened and she smiled at him.

"Hi."

"Hi, yourself. How are you feeling?"

"Better every day, I think. I wish I could get up and walk around some. I'm getting tired of this couch." She huffed out a breath.

"I'm sure you are. I could sit you out on the back some in the morning when we're outside there. I don't think it would be a good idea for you to sit outside without one of us close by."

He watched the light fade from her eyes. He wanted to take the words back that had dulled her excitement. Still, they were the truth.

She had to know it was too dangerous for her to sit outside alone, especially when she couldn't defend herself or run.

"Maybe when you're doing chores around the house tomorrow. I'd like that. I'm tired of looking at these four walls."

"We fixed a hole in the fence out in the pasture. I don't think we lost any of your cows, though. They probably just hadn't found it yet." Garrett felt tongue-tied around her now that he was there. He didn't know what to talk about.

"That's something I haven't checked in a while. I just haven't had the time with getting in the garden and putting things up for the winter. Thanks for checking for me."

"Ronnie, Brice told me he suggested that you let us find you a good man to settle here with you. How do you really feel about it?"

"I don't know. I don't think I want a complete stranger coming here. I told him I think I can take care of myself. I've been doing it anyway."

"What happens if you get hurt again? You need some help, Ronnie." Garrett lifted her legs, being careful of her left ankle, and sat down on the couch, cushioning her feet in his lap.

"Um, I-I don't know. I just have to be careful and not get hurt. Oh, Garrett, I don't know what to do." There were tears in her eyes now.

Garrett felt terrible for bringing it all up again. He wanted to see how she would feel about them staying with her, most importantly, him.

"Would you be more comfortable with us?"

She looked up into his eyes and smiled. "Yes, I would. I'm used to you and Brice. I trust you two."

Garrett slowly let out the breath he had been holding. She had included him in her trust. He'd talk to Brice about it later.

"Are you saying you might be willing to stay and, and well, stay with me?" Her voice trembled.

"I don't know. I thought I would see if you were comfortable with us or not and talk to Brice. I'm not sure how he feels about sticking around in one place."

"I understand."

Brice walked in with a glass of tea, an odd look on his face. Garrett figured he had overheard. Well, he was going to talk to him about staying anyway. It just meant he didn't have to bring it up. Brice would do that the first time they were alone.

"Garrett, can you help me in the kitchen for a minute?"

Well, it looked like he wasn't going to wait around until they were alone. Brice was going to make time.

Chapter Six

Garrett followed Brice into the kitchen and then back outside. Evidently, he wasn't going to take any chance that Ronnie would overhear them. This didn't bode well.

"Did I hear you right? Did you just offer for us to stay with her—permanently?"

"I told her I'd talk to you about it. She said she was comfortable with us and wouldn't be with anyone else, Brice."

"We've talked some about this, and I thought we agreed we weren't ready to settle down right now."

"You said you didn't think you were. And if you're not, I understand, but I'm seriously thinking about it, if she'll have me. I guess there's a chance she won't as she's so uneasy around me anyway."

"Dammit, Garrett. We've been together since college. You're talking about splitting up." Brice stuck his hands on his hips and looked up as if studying the sky for an answer.

"I don't want to split up. I want you to stay here with us. She's more comfortable around you, anyway. You like her. I can tell. You can't tell me you haven't jerked off in the shower any more than I can."

"That doesn't a true relationship make, Garrett. It's just sex."

"Which we're not getting now anyway, and we both still care about her. She's interesting to talk to and is obviously a hard worker. She's got a body that keeps my dick hard all day long. Why wouldn't you want to at least think about it?"

"I have thought about it. Fuck, Garrett. I just don't know if I can settle down or not. We've been on the road for too long."

"I think you can. You've settled here for this long and haven't acted like it's been a hardship. Why not stick around for a little longer and see if you can?"

Garrett watched Brice for any clue as to what he would do. He gave nothing away on his face. He rarely did.

"I'll think about it, but that's all I'll promise right now."

"That's good enough for me. But, Brice, if she'll have me, I'm staying."

"Fuck." Brice headed for the barn. "I'm going to get started on that fucking cow."

Garrett watched him go and sighed. He didn't want to lose his friend, but he was afraid he was falling in love with Ronnie and didn't want to leave her. He just hoped she would learn to care about him and not be so skittish around him.

He turned around and walked back into the house. He hesitated before walking back into the living room. He wasn't sure what to tell her. Coward that he was, he decided to start supper instead. He would think on it a little longer and then talk to her again. Maybe Brice would have decided something by then as well.

Brice didn't come back in until he had supper ready and on the table. He decided to bring Ronnie into the kitchen to eat tonight. She wouldn't be up for long, but it would be a change in scenery for her.

While Brice cleaned up, Garrett hurried into the other room to see about carrying Ronnie into the kitchen. She was staring at the fire when he walked back into the room. She jerked her head up and smiled at him. His heart stuttered in his chest.

"Thought you might like to sit at the table for supper tonight."

"Thanks, that would be great." She pushed off the couch with one hand and stood on one leg.

"Whoa, there. You'll hurt yourself." He quickly picked her up and carried her into the other room and settled her at the table.

Brice walked over and checked her wrist. "Looks better. In fact, you look better sitting up."

"I feel better sitting up." She smiled at him.

Garrett watched them, hoping Brice wouldn't say anything to dim her smile. It brightened her face despite the bruises still evident there. He gathered up the dishes and served them. Brice kept up a running dialogue about little things going on around the farm and even had her laugh at his daily battle with the cow.

As soon as she was finished, Garrett gathered her up in his arms and carried her to the couch again. He didn't want her to wear herself out.

Brice didn't say anything when he walked back in. He gathered up the dishes and helped Garrett wash them then put them away. He couldn't tell what was going through Brice's mind. His friend had clamped down on his expressions so that he didn't have a clue.

Damn, he hadn't wanted to drive a wedge between them. He only wanted to look at settling down. He should have talked to Brice about it before now. He'd shied away from broaching the subject for just this reason.

"I'm going to go ahead and take a shower. I'm nasty." Brice headed up the stairs, leaving Garrett alone with Ronnie.

"Where was Brice going?" she asked with a puzzled expression.

"He went to take his shower. He said he was so dirty he could smell himself."

"Oh."

"Soon as he finishes, I'll help you get in the tub if you want."

"I'd love that. I feel so nasty just taking sink baths." She picked at her shirt.

"Well, your stitches are out of your head, so Brice said you could get your head wet now. You can even wash your hair if you like." Garrett enjoyed seeing her face light up at the idea.

They talked about things around the ranch. She explained that she had a garden each year. She lived off the canned goods she could find and what she put up from the garden.

"I don't grow much because I can't dig up much ground for planting. I wanted to try and get a garden tractor, but I'm scared to drive to one of the abandoned towns around here. I'm scared someone will catch me."

"It's best if you don't do anything like that alone. You really don't need to be out and about alone anyway."

"It's so unfair!" she exclaimed.

"What's unfair?" Brice walked back down the stairs into the living room.

"That I can't go anywhere alone. I feel like a convict on a chain."

"I'm sorry. I wish it wasn't like that, but the world is different from how it used to be, and there isn't anything we can do about it." Brice laid a hand on her shoulder and gently squeezed it.

Garrett watched how he touched her. He had to feel something for her. He touched her too often and got all quiet with her. Brice was only fooling himself if he thought he wasn't affected by her. His friend might not realize it yet, but he would. He cared about her just as much as Garrett did. All he had to do was figure out a way to prove it to him.

* * * *

Ronnie enjoyed talking with the two men. Both of them were interesting and could be funny. Brice was obviously highly intelligent. Garrett was a big teddy bear. He looked all rough and scary, but he really wasn't. She liked both of them for different reasons. With Brice, she felt cared for and knew he could figure out any problem. With Garrett, she felt protected and safe. He would fix anything he could.

If either one of them volunteered to stay, she'd take them up on it and try her best to relax and handle the sex part. Since her body seemed to think it wanted them, then maybe she could hold back the fear and discomfort from them.

"You about ready for your bath?" Garrett asked, standing up.

"That would be great, thanks. I'm getting tired."

He picked her up and carried her up the stairs.

"I'm going to make sure all the doors are locked, and I'll be right up," Brice called up to them.

Garrett sat Ronnie on the bed and hurried to run her water. She hoped she could wash her hair without too much trouble. It would feel so much better to have clean hair. The men had worked hard at getting the dried blood out of it earlier in the week, but nothing felt better than a good head scrubbing. Then she remembered her bum wrist. Damn. What was she going to do?

"Okay, I have the water ready. Let's get you undressed and in the tub." Garrett helped her by unbuttoning the shirt, then had her lie back so he could pull her panties off. Then he picked her up and carried her to the tub. He let her slowly get used to the water with her feet before settling her back in the tub.

"It's a little cold. I'm not sure I can wash my hair."

"I'll run down and heat up a bucket of water on the stove. It's too bad the hot water heater isn't gas. Maybe we can find one and switch it out."

She latched on to that statement as a positive indication that he was thinking about staying. She began to wash using her good hand and managed to get most of her washing done by the time he returned with a bucket of hot water. He added it slowly to the water at her feet until she felt warm all over.

"Thanks, that is so much better."

"Would you like me to get your back?" Garrett asked her.

"Um, thanks, that would be nice. I can't reach it.

"Lean up." He lathered up the cloth and scrubbed her back in a brisk wash. It felt delicious.

"Okay, why don't you lean back and get your head wet while you rinse off your back. I'll scrub your hair for you since you only have one hand."

Ronnie let him lean her back and submerged her head up to her ears. She closed her eyes, not wanting to see him staring at her breasts. He seemed to try not to stare, but he still did at times. He was a man, after all.

When he helped her sit back up, she kept her eyes closed to keep the water from getting in them. He poured some shampoo on her head and began to gently message it into her scalp and then all down the rest of her hair. He shampooed it a bit awkwardly at first, but soon got the hang of it. By the time he had finished, she felt like a new person.

Once she was finished rinsing off, Garrett handed her a small towel to wipe her face then helped her stand on one foot once out of the tub. He took a towel and dried her off from head to toe. He rubbed her hair until it was no longer wet, only damp.

"Garrett?"

"Yeah, baby." He patted her dry over her breasts, obviously trying to keep from being too personal.

"I don't think I can stand up long enough to dry my hair all the way. Can you carry me to the bedroom?"

"Of course." He wrapped the towel around her chest before he picked her up and carried her to the bedroom, where he sat her on the foot of the bed.

He used a dry towel to rub at her hair. She kept her shoulders forward and let him work on her hair. With only one hand, she wouldn't have been able to dry it herself. It would have had to air-dry, and that might lead to pneumonia. She couldn't afford that on top of everything else.

"Want me to spell you?" Brice asked from the bed, where he'd been reclining.

"Sure. I'll move the light closer." Garrett grabbed the kerosene lamp from the bathroom and sat it on the dresser.

She noticed that Brice worked differently from Garrett. Where Garrett rubbed on a large area, Brice took small sections and dried them before moving on to another small area of hair. Between Brice and Garrett, her hair was essentially dry within a matter of an hour. It normally took her a good two or so hours to dry her hair alone.

"I bet you feel better with a clean head," Brice commented.

"I really do. I was beginning to feel like a mud puddle. Thanks for helping me dry my hair."

"I didn't mind. You have lovely hair. It's soft and thick."

Garrett ran a comb through it as they talked.

"Have you tried to walk on your foot at all yet?" Brice asked.

"No, I move it around every once in a while, but I haven't tried to stand on it. I didn't think I should try it alone."

"No, you don't need to do that alone. We'll check it out tomorrow. Give you one more night to rest it up. Your wrist is still not well, though. It's too swollen. Can you wiggle all your fingers okay?"

"Actually, I can move them pretty easy without too much discomfort. It's just when I try and make a fist or grab for something before I remember that it's hurt that it really gives me trouble."

"Don't irritate it. I'm leaning toward you having a broken bone in there somewhere. I just don't have a way of telling, and there's nothing we can do anyway." Brice stood up and walked back toward his side of the bed. "I'm going to turn in. You two going to talk all night, or come to bed?"

Garrett chuckled and picked her up to ease her into the bed beneath the covers. She felt Brice's leg next to hers, but she willed herself not to move.

"I'm going to take my shower now," Garrett said, taking the lamp with him.

When he closed the door, it threw the room into darkness. Ronnie could hear her own heartbeat in her ears and felt as if Brice could hear it as well. She tried to slow it down, but it rushed on anyway. Was she afraid of the dark or uneasy with Brice in the bed and the lights out?

"You still awake over there, Ronnie?"

"Yeah, it's so dark in here."

"It was cloudy when I came in earlier. Looks like snow."

"I hope not. That just adds to the chores," Ronnie said with a sigh.

"How so?" Brice asked.

"You have to shovel paths to the barn and the chicken coop and the pasture to feed everyone."

"Hadn't thought about that." Brice moved in the bed, bringing more of his body flush against her side.

"I wish I wasn't like this. I could help with everything, and you wouldn't be in this predicament you're in." Ronnie sighed.

"What predicament are you talking about?"

"Having to take care of me." Ronnie couldn't help the bitterness from creeping into her voice.

"We don't have to take care of you," he said. "We do it because we want to. I've learned a lot in these last few days. More than I ever knew about farms at all. It's been good for me."

"If you say so. I can't imagine your being okay with a change in plans to the extent this changed yours."

"So you know me that well, do you?" he asked with a smile in his voice.

"Well, you seem like someone who makes plans and sticks to them no matter what."

"Thanks, I think." He chuckled and ran a hand down her arm to her hand.

She let him hold it. He was very careful not to hurt her sore wrist. Ronnie wasn't sure how to react to his holding her hand like a boyfriend. She pretended like he always did it and didn't make any move to remove her hand from his. Neither did she stop his other hand from exploring her breasts.

Ronnie couldn't catch her breath. It came in quick pants as Brice slowly caressed her breasts. At first, he merely touched them, then he began to stroke them as if petting a favorite dog. When he brushed against her nipple, she nearly died right there. Never had something felt so good.

Garrett walked in with a towel around his waist, whistling. The tune he was whistling faltered for a few seconds when he saw that Brice was playing with her breasts. To his credit, he didn't say anything. He merely dropped the towel, set the lamp on the bedside table, and climbed into bed with them. He turned so that he could watch Brice's fingers slowly tease her nipples.

The sensation of Brice's fingers on her nipples elicited a moan from her she hadn't known existed. He seemed to take it as a go-ahead for more exploring. He kissed her breasts. Then he sucked in a nipple and tongued all around it.

Ronnie felt as if her body would explode, it felt so damn good. She pushed her breast up into his mouth. Then she felt another mouth at her other breast. She opened her eyes and looked down to find Garrett at her other breast. The sensation of two hot mouths was almost her undoing. She wrapped her arms around the two men, cursing when her left wrist wouldn't let her grab ahold of Brice's head.

Slowly they let her nipples pop from their mouths. They licked their lips and stared down into her face as if asking for permission to go farther. She didn't know whether to say yes and try sex, or say no and wish she had later. The worst that could happen was that she would hate it and beg them to stop. But maybe, just maybe, she would actually like it.

Chapter Seven

Garrett gazed down at Ronnie with hungry eyes. She couldn't believe she had let them touch her breasts, much less suck on them. She could tell they were asking for more. Could she go further? She drew in a deep breath and nodded her head. It was all the encouragement they needed, evidently, since they immediately began exploring her body.

One minute they were waiting on some sign from her, and the next, they were driving her wild with need. She'd never felt such need before. It begged for more, and she didn't know how to ask for it.

Brice kissed her neck and shoulder and nibbled around her jawline. He covered her face, neck, and shoulders in open-mouthed kisses. She longed to taste him and moved her head in that direction for a kiss.

At the same time, Garrett had returned to her breasts and was lathing them with his tongue and lips. He moved from one to the other and then back again, as if unable to decide where to concentrate. He finally settled on one and used his fingers to stimulate her other nipple. The sensation of his mouth sucking pulled on things low in her body. Her cunt pulsed and dripped juices.

At last Brice reached her mouth with his lips and kissed her. It was a soft, tentative kiss at first, but soon grew until he was licking along the seam of her lips. She opened for him and he filled her mouth with his tongue, rubbing it up and down hers as he wound a hand in her hair. He didn't pull it so much as anchor her with it. She moaned into his kiss and he deepened it.

Her breasts were on fire from Garrett's mouth and fingers. He changed from one nipple to the other with his mouth, and then back again. Sometimes he nipped at them, and sometimes he sucked. At the same time, his fingers pulled and pinched the opposite breast. Ronnie wanted to grab his head and hold him to her breast for some reason. She wanted him to swallow her, but knew he couldn't.

Instead, he began to slide farther down the bed, laying kisses along her abdomen and pelvis until he reached her pussy. She was so involved in Brice's kisses that she jumped and squealed when Garrett licked her sodden cunt. Never had anyone put their mouth down there.

"Oh, God!" She pulled back from Brice to breathe.

"Do you like what Garrett's doing to you, baby?" Brice whispered in her ear.

"I-I don't know. I've never had anyone kiss me down there."

"How does it feel to you?" Brice nipped at her earlobe, then licked it.

"Good. It feels naughty, but good."

"Garrett loves eating sweet pussies like yours. I bet he's digging his tongue deep right now, isn't he, Ronnie."

"Oh, yes, he's licking me all over, and even inside. I want to touch him. Can I touch him?"

"Grab him, baby. Let him know how good that feels." Brice moved away from her some to give her room, but he didn't let go of her hair.

Ronnie leaned forward and grabbed Garrett's head as he stuck his tongue deep inside of her. She nearly screamed at the intense feel of it. Yet it wasn't enough. She wanted something else, something more.

Brice slipped behind her and let her lean back against him. He nuzzled her neck while fondling her breasts at the same time. Ronnie loved being the center of their attention and all the wild feelings inside of her. She felt like a kernel of popcorn, ready to explode, but didn't know what that would mean.

"I need," she gasped.

"Need what, Ronnie?" Brice asked her as he pinched and twisted and tugged on her nipples.

"More, I don't know, something more."

"Garrett, she wants more, man. Give her something more."

Garrett entered her pussy with a finger and began to slowly move it in and out as he licked all around her clit. He brushed over it, and she groaned and bucked at the hot sensation. She wanted more of that. When he licked close again, she tried to follow his talented tongue with her pussy, but he avoided her.

"Please, Garrett."

Instead of giving her what she asked for, he inserted two fingers inside of her and began pumping them in and out at a faster pace than before. Fire began to heat the inside of her body. Her blood sang through her veins. It raced around in circles waiting for something.

Then he curled his fingers up and brushed against the top of her cunt until he located a spot inside that had her jerking from the bed. It felt like electricity arced across her body as he gently brushed over it every few seconds. Her face grew hot, as did the rest of her body, and she knew something was about to happen. She just didn't know what. She wanted to explode inside but didn't know how to make it happen without using her own hand.

"You're going to come for us, Ronnie. You're going to come all over Garrett's face and give him all of your sweet honey." Brice continued playing with her nipples and nibbled her neck.

When she couldn't be still any longer, Garrett placed a hand on her pelvis and held her down as he pumped two fingers in and out of her and licked her juices from her pussy lips. As if on cue, he curled his fingers to stroke her hot spot and sucked her clit into his mouth all at the same time. Brice pinched her nipples and bit her shoulder. Ronnie could do nothing but scream out her release and explode. Fireworks detonated in her blood and sparked behind her eyes. She couldn't breathe past it all.

Garrett slowly let her down with soft, easy licks until she was lying propped against Brice, panting and gasping all at the same time. Garrett looked up her body at her with a satisfied expression. His face was still wet with her juices.

"Ronnie, you are so beautiful when you come. I could watch you come for hours." Brice wrapped his arms around her and gently squeezed her.

"I've never, could never." She couldn't put it into words.

"Climaxed? Are you saying you've never had a climax before?" Brice asked.

"No, only when I touched myself."

"Ronnie, baby, I want to fuck you right now so badly I might not make it inside of you. Will you trust us enough to let us try that?" Garrett looked to be holding his breath, waiting on her answer.

Could she do it? She did trust them and honestly didn't think they would hurt her, but could she handle letting them fuck her when always before, it had hurt?

"I don't know if I can do it or not, but I'll try." She swallowed hard and waited for him to stick his dick inside of her.

Instead, he backed off the bed and turned the lamp up a little bit so that she could see him. He was gloriously aroused and larger than she had originally thought. There was no way he would ever fit inside of her. He was too big of a man.

"Garrett?"

"Shh, baby. He'll fit."

She had nearly forgotten that Brice was holding her.

"Relax, Ronnie. I'd never hurt you for anything. Let me do all the work." Garrett knelt on the bed and lifted her hips to align his massive cock with her slit.

She felt him drag himself up and down in her juices before he began to press forward. She panicked at first when he began to push into her. Brice kept whispering in her ear how beautiful she looked and how good it was going to feel. She almost missed it when he finally popped inside her pussy with the massive head of his cock.

"There we go. You're so fucking tight, baby. Hold on to Brice. I'm going to fuck myself into you."

She grasped Brice's forearm with her good hand and tensed up. Brice kissed her and told her to relax.

"He'll feel so good when he fills you up, Ronnie. Just let go and let him inside."

Garrett slowly backed out then pushed back in, over and over, until he had managed to lodge himself all the way inside of her hot pussy. He bent forward and touched their moist foreheads together as he rested and allowed her to adjust to his massive girth.

"You okay, baby?" he asked.

"I'm so full. You're all the way inside me, aren't you?"

"All the way. Are you ready to move now?" Garrett wiggled his dick a little, and she smiled at the sensation it made inside of her.

"Fuck me, Garrett. Make me come again."

Brice moved out from behind her and lay next to them. As Garrett began to pull almost all the way out, he sucked and nibbled on her breasts. Then Garrett was pushing back inside of her again. Over and over, deeper and deeper, faster and faster, until Ronnie thought she would die from the pleasure racing in her veins.

"Brice, I'm not going to last, man." Garrett's voice sounded strained as he pummeled her pussy with his dick.

"I've got her, man." Brice sucked her nipple deep into his mouth and tongued it while slipping his hand between her and Garrett to rub her clit.

Ronnie screamed as her cunt exploded. She felt her cunt muscles squeeze down hard on Garrett's cock. Then he was coming with her, and she felt him fill her with his cum before collapsing over her. She struggled to breathe and then laughed when Brice reached over and pushed Garrett off of her.

Long minutes later, a very exhausted but obviously satisfied Garrett rolled out of bed and headed for the bathroom. He returned a few minutes later with a wet cloth he used to clean her up. No one had ever done that for her before. Then again, no one had ever made her come, not once, but twice in one night. She looked over at Brice.

"What about you, Brice? Isn't it your turn?" she asked.

"You're tired, Ronnie. You're still recovering from your wreck. I don't have to come tonight. I will another time." He pulled the covers over her after snuggling up against her.

"I want to make you feel good, too. You and Garrett made me feel so good." She turned to face him and curled her hands in his chest hair. "Please, let me make you feel good too. I won't sleep, thinking about it."

"Ronnie, baby. You don't have to do this."

"I know. And that's probably part of the reason why I want to. You're not making me." She shoved the covers down and tugged on his thermals to push them down his hips so she could get to his cock. When he sprang up from the soft material, she smiled.

"What's so funny down there?" Brice sounded a bit put out that she was all but giggling over his cock.

"It's just that it's so big. I mean, I knew Garrett would be big because he's a really big man, but you're not as big as he is, but your cock is just as thick."

"Thanks, I think," he said with a frown.

Ronnie took that moment to lick his dick from base to tip and back down again. It jumped in her hands. She couldn't get one hand around it, so she used both hands and held him firm while she explored his cock. She licked him around and around until a drop of pre-cum pearled in the slit at the top. She stuck out her tongue and tasted it. His taste exploded on her tongue like a banquet. His salty essence was spicy as well. She delved into the slit for more. He hissed and dug his fingers in her scalp.

Ronnie was careful not to put too much pressure on her left wrist as she took the head of his cock into her mouth and sucked. He growled low in his throat as she sucked her way down his thick stalk until she couldn't go any farther. She swallowed around him and moaned when he pulled on her hair.

"Fuck! Do that again, baby. That felt so damn good." Brice's voice came out all strained and raspy.

She hummed around his thick dick and felt him jerk in her mouth. He liked that. She pulled back up, letting her teeth graze him just a bit as she did. Then she sucked around the crown and swallowed back down him again.

She slipped her good hand into his thermals and cupped his balls. They were heavy and hot to touch. She rolled them in her hand as she suckled his cock. The harder she sucked, the higher his balls drew up. She could tell he was close because he was thrusting into her mouth now as if he couldn't help it. She raked his balls with her nails and he exploded in her mouth. She swallowed down the cum he gave her until it was all gone, then licked him clean.

"Fuck, Ronnie, that was so damn good. I don't know if I'll ever catch my breath again." He panted as he lay back against the pillow.

"Come on, Ronnie. You need to rest now, baby. We've worn you out." Garrett pulled her closer to him as Brice adjusted his thermals and got back under the covers.

"The light," Ronnie whispered, already almost asleep.

"I've got it," Garrett said as she closed her eyes and drifted deep into sleep.

* * * *

"You still awake, Brice?" Garrett needed to know where he stood with his friend.

"Yeah, I'm still flying high after that fucking blow job."

"She's something else, isn't she?" Garrett hoped Brice was at least considering staying.

"Yeah, she is."

"What made you start loving on her?" Garrett asked.

"She didn't jump away from me when we touched accidently. I thought I'd see how far I could get with her. She seemed determined to not pull away. One thing led to another and the next thing I know, we're both sucking her sweet tits."

"Man, she tastes like warm honey. I could make a meal off of her," Garrett admitted.

"You're planning on staying, aren't you?"

"Yeah, I am. I was hoping you would, too. You see that she has accepted both of us."

"I just don't know, Garrett. I hate to settle down and get her used to me, then realize I can't stay and leave her. I know she'll still have you, but it's bound to hurt."

"Hurt you, too," Garrett said, knowing that was the real reason he wasn't going to stay.

"Yeah, it would hurt me to leave both of you once I stayed for a while."

"You don't have to go. You haven't been antsy since you've been here, that I can tell." Garrett ran a hand down Ronnie's arm, needing the touch to help stave off the fear of losing his best friend.

"It doesn't mean that a few weeks or maybe months down the line I won't get that way. We've been on the road for years, Garrett. I'm glad you can settle down, but I just don't think I can right now." Brice's voice faded.

"Hell, fine. I understand. You know you have a place here anytime you want to come back, or just visit."

"I know. I'll keep in touch. Besides, I'm not gone yet. I'm going to stay around until she's on her feet."

Garrett sighed and nuzzled his nose against Ronnie's neck. He would worry about Brice by himself, but he couldn't make his friend stick around. Still, as much as he knew he would miss Brice, he also knew his place was here now. He felt it in his bones. It felt like home to him. He could see himself grow old here. Maybe raise some kids. He just wished that Brice wouldn't be so hardheaded about it and leave them.

Chapter Eight

The next few days, they all worked long and hard to get things done so that they had more light left at night to get things done in the house. It had snowed a few inches, but not much more, and it hadn't caused any problems with the animals or doing chores.

Brice supervised Ronnie standing on her foot for the first time, and agreed she could limp around some in the house for short periods of time. She pushed it with him, and he'd jumped on her twice for overdoing it. Sometimes she felt like he really cared about her, and other times, not so much.

"Brice?" Ronnie limped into the kitchen, where he was stowing the milk and eggs from that morning's chores.

"Yeah, baby?" He turned and looked at her.

"Why don't you want me?"

"Why would you think that, Ronnie?" He stopped washing his hands and stared at her.

"You never fuck me. You let me suck you off and you jack off in the shower. Don't say you don't. But you haven't fucked me." She sat down at the table and propped her bad foot on top of her other one.

"Ronnie, you know I'm not going to stay. I just didn't think it was fair to you or to Garrett if I fucked you then left. I mean, what if you get pregnant? You wouldn't know whose child it was."

"It wouldn't matter to me. I want you to stay, Brice. At least stay part of the year with us. You can stay here in the winter and go scavenging in the summer months. Wouldn't that work for you?"

"I'm sorry, Ronnie, but I can't. I'll probably leave in another week. You're just about ready to be discharged from my medical care now."

He tried to tease her, but she wasn't falling for it. He wasn't going to stick around any longer than he had to. He didn't care about her like Garrett did. It hurt. It hurt a lot. She cared about Brice just as much as she cared about Garrett. Knowing he didn't feel the same way made her feel bad, so she got angry.

"Fine. You can go whenever you get ready to. I can handle the chickens and the cow. My wrist isn't that bad. I can probably out-milk you one-handed anyway."

She stormed off as fast as her sore ankle would let her go. She carefully climbed the stairs and searched through her things until she found clothes to put on. She still couldn't stand the bra around her chest, so she went braless, but she dressed in her normal clothes. Getting her foot into the boot was nerve-racking, but she finally managed it.

She found Garrett out working on one of the barrels that she used to catch rainwater for the garden.

"Hey, baby. What are you doing out here?"

"Tired of being in the house. I need to get back on my feet so I can take over when Brice leaves. I doubt he'll be here more than another few days."

"What makes you think that?" Garrett stood up and stared down at her.

"He as much as said so a while ago." She couldn't stop the tears from falling.

"Oh, fuck, Ronnie, don't cry." Garrett wrapped his arms around her and pulled her in tight to his body. She breathed in the male scent that she so loved.

"I'll be okay. I'm just pissed that he's leaving."

"I know. He'll come back and see us," Garrett told her.

"Do you really believe that?" she asked.

"Yeah, I do. He'll visit and then he'll realize he's tired of all the traveling and he'll come back and settle in with us."

"Maybe."

Ronnie wasn't so sure he would show back up at all. He had that look about him that said he was ready to make a run for it. He felt trapped. She was sure she was the reason for it, too. Garrett was losing his best friend because of her.

"I'm going to go back inside and skim the milk. I'll see you at lunch." Ronnie felt like a heel.

That night after supper, they sat in the living room in front of the fire, talking about the weather and what they thought it would do next.

"I suspect it will snow again by the end of the week," Ronnie told them. It's been too dry lately, and we usually have a foot by now."

"We need supplies if we're going to get through the winter with me living here now. Brice, want to make a run to Sky Line and gather up some things? We can pick up another truck for here while we are out." Garrett hugged Ronnie against him.

"That's probably a good idea." Brice nodded and stretched his feet out in front of him. "You need some supplies, and Ronnie needs clothes. She doesn't have anything in her drawers."

"Hey, I'm here, you know." She resented it when they talked about her like she wasn't even in the room.

"Sorry, baby." Garrett looked at her. "He's right, though. You don't have decent clothes, and especially not for winter."

"Can you manage the morning chores alone if we go tomorrow while the weather is holding?"

"Yeah, I can handle them. My wrist is just a little stiff still. Nothing that some regular exercise wouldn't help."

"You going to be okay here by yourself?" Garrett asked.

"She'll be fine, Garrett," Brice said. "We better head to bed if we're going to get up early and leave."

"I'm going to make out a list of things I know we need and leave it on the kitchen table for you in the morning. I'll be up in a few minutes." Ronnie stood up and slipped out of Garrett's grip to find something to write on.

She took the lamp with her and laughed to herself. The men would have to make it upstairs in the dark or light another lamp.

She found a sheet of tablet paper and a pen in a drawer and sat at the kitchen table to make out her list. There were so many things they could use, but she narrowed it down to the things they needed the most, like canned goods. She refused to acknowledge the tears running down her face. Brice would leave after this trip, she was sure of it.

Ronnie finished the list and sat it on the table with the pen on top of it. Then she checked the fire to be sure it was banked, and climbed the stairs. She doused the light as she opened the door and let her eyes adjust to the dark before setting the lamp on the dresser. She stripped down to nothing and climbed in the bed between the two men. Garrett immediately snuggled next to her, but Brice remained on his side of the bed.

* * * *

Brice tossed and turned all night long, thinking about leaving. He wanted to stay so badly but knew it was for the best, because he didn't want to become too attached to Ronnie and then get the wanderlust and leave her. It would break both of their hearts. Leaving now was better in the long run.

Finally, around four thirty, he climbed out of bed and grabbed his clothes. He dressed hurriedly in the bathroom, then tiptoed downstairs. By the time Garrett made it downstairs, he had the coffee and some sandwiches made for their trip.

"You're up early." Garrett took the cup Brice handed him.

"Couldn't sleep. Guess I was antsy about getting on the road."

"I'm ready to start out whenever you are," Garrett said in a strange voice.

Brice looked at him but didn't see anything in his friend's expression to explain the slight bite in his tone.

"Ronnie's list is over on the table." Brice pointed it out for him.

Garrett picked it up and stuffed it in his coat pocket.

"Help me remember gloves and a scarf for her."

"Will do." Brice unlocked the front door then locked it back behind them. He climbed into the cab of the truck and waited on Garrett to do the same.

"Do you think she'll be okay here alone?"

"She's been alone for the last three years. She'll be fine."

Brice felt uneasy leaving, though, and figured it was just because he'd been there for nearly three weeks now. He'd begun to put down roots, and that was why he needed to get going again. Today would be a good dry run for him.

They pulled into Sky Line around eight that morning. They decided to top off the fuel first, and then locate some stores to explore. Brice decided to head across town to the other side, where fewer people ventured. There were more wolf packs in that area.

They stopped at a Super Kmart and found a way inside where someone had already broken the lock in the back of the store.

They loaded up on items from Ronnie's list and stacked them in boxes in the back. When they got to the clothing, they chose work jeans, shirts, and boots for her, but frilly underwear for underneath. They found several pairs of gloves and scarves, as well as thermals that were pink. Brice figured she would get a kick out of them.

"She's going to love the underwear," Garrett said. "We should look for a few new coats, too. Yours is already falling apart, and I noticed that the only one Ronnie has is torn in several places."

They located a sporting goods store where there were a few things left. They managed to each find a coat and two for Ronnie. All the ammunition and guns were gone, but they located some knives.

"It wouldn't hurt for Ronnie to have one on her at all times," Brice said.

They drove over to the car dealership where Garrett picked out a SUV in silver. They located a couple more stores and filled up the back of the SUV as well. By the time they were ready to get back on the road, it was nearly four in the afternoon. It was already getting dark. They needed to get back to the house.

Brice led the way. He thought about Ronnie most of the way home. Garrett would take good care of her, and she'd eventually forget about him. He wasn't sure it would be a good idea to go back once he left. Maybe he'd drop them off some supplies now and then when they were asleep.

Why was he so hung up over leaving them? Sure, he was going to miss Garrett. They'd been together through everything for nearly ten years now. Knowing he might not ever see him again weighed heavily on him.

Then there was how he felt about Ronnie. He cared about her. He knew he did, but sometimes it felt like more, and that scared him. He'd never wanted to be responsible for another's happiness. That was one of the reasons he enjoyed sharing women with Garrett. Garrett saw to their softer needs. Brice made them feel good about their body and relaxed around them, but it was Garrett who catered to their feminine side, that need to cuddle and talk afterward.

When they pulled up into the drive around seven thirty, the house was dark. There didn't even seem to be a fire in the fireplace, as there was no smoke coming from the chimney. Unease slithered across his skin as he climbed out of the truck.

"Brice?"

"I see it. Let's go around to the back and come in that way."

They eased around the back of the house to the kitchen door. Garrett unlocked the door and they quietly entered the house. Brice couldn't hear a sound. He led the way to the living room with nothing looking out of place that he could see. By the time he made it upstairs, he had just about convinced himself they were worried for no reason. She'd just let the fire die out by accident or couldn't pick up wood with her bum hand.

The only thing was, she wasn't in the bedroom or the bathroom. They checked each and every room upstairs, and then started all over again.

"Hell, Brice. Someone's got her."

"Calm down. Let's look around outside. She may be late doing chores or something."

Brice didn't think so, but he couldn't stomach the alternative. It had been his idea for them to go to Sky Line and leave her on her own. He should have known better.

They searched the backyard, the chicken coop, and finally the barn. Just as they were about to give up, a noise in the loft and the fall of hay alerted them that something or someone was up in the hay. Brice put his finger over his lips so that Garrett could see him. Then he climbed up the ladder and came face-to-face with the business end of a shotgun and Ronnie behind it. Hay stuck out of her hair all over, and she had some stuck in her shirt as well.

"Brice? Is that really you? Where's Garrett?" Her voice shook.

"He's right down here. What are you doing up in the loft?" Brice had a feeling he wasn't going to like the answer.

"I—" she began.

"Come on down here. Let's go to the house and start a fire where we'll be warm to discuss this," Garrett called up the ladder.

As soon as she was down on the floor, she threw herself in Garrett's arms. He hugged and kissed her and told her everything was fine now. Brice had to swallow down his jealousy that she'd run to Garrett. He wasn't going to be around. This is the very reason he was getting ready to leave.

They walked into the house, shivering in the cold. Brice gathered wood and began setting the fire ablaze. Soon the room was toasty once again. They settled on the couch, with Garrett cuddling Ronnie. Brice provided warmth on the other side of her, but nothing more.

"After you left, I milked the cow and gathered the eggs. I was bringing in wood for the fire, when a man drove up in a truck and asked where my men were. I told him you were gone to scavenge and would be back soon. He looked at me and said, 'You don't really have a man, do you?' I was scared enough I didn't know what to do," she said.

"What did you do?" Garrett asked.

"I told him to get lost before you got home. He pushed his way inside and chased me out the back door. I ran, but couldn't do much on with my ankle, and he caught me. He dragged me back to his truck and tried to get me in it. I bit him, and he hit me, but not very hard. I managed to kick him in the nuts. He rolled around on the ground, and I kicked him in the head. It knocked him out."

"What did you do with him?" Brice asked.

"Nothing. I ran and got the gun and hid. I heard the truck start up sometime later and leave. I was too scared to come out, though. I didn't think you would ever get back."

"I'm sorry, Ronnie. I should have known better than to leave you like that. One of us should have stayed with you. Or better yet, you could have gone with us," Brice told her.

"I couldn't have left the cow and chickens untended to, and you all needed to leave early." She continued to hang on to Garrett.

Brice had to stamp down the angry, jealous man he didn't know was inside of him.

"Well, you're going to have to go with him when he goes looking for supplies in the future. You can't stay by yourself anymore." Brice didn't budge on this. She needed two men. One to scavenge, and one to watch out for her.

"Garrett, we can work it out later. What did you get this time? Do we need to unload it so no one gets it?" she asked.

"Yeah, we can leave the stuff in Garrett's SUV and unload the stuff out of the back of my truck." Brice walked through the house to the half bath downstairs. "I'll meet you outside."

Brice closed the door to the half bath and leaned against it after locking it. He felt as close to crying as he'd felt since the year of catastrophes five years earlier. He'd almost lost Ronnie by insisting they go to Sky Line, knowing she'd already had trouble with men around the house. He'd been so ready to get back on the road, he'd totally disregarded her safety. He didn't deserve a woman like her. If he couldn't take care of her, he shouldn't be allowed to hold her.

It was time for him to move on before he endangered her again somehow. He'd help them unload and put everything away the next day, and then leave the following day at dawn. Tonight, he would hold Ronnie in his arms so he had something to remember and keep him warm on the coming cold nights. Even though he knew he didn't deserve to hold her, he needed it to know that she was okay and still there. Garrett would never have forgiven him if something had happened to her.

Chapter Nine

They worked all day on unloading and putting away all the groceries and supplies they'd managed to find. Although she assured them she loved her new clothes, she was totally embarrassed by the underwear. It was frilly, and not something she was used to wearing. She was glad that Garrett had known what sizes she needed. The good thing about her size was that not a lot of people wore what she wore.

She had just put away the last of the clothing when Garrett walked upstairs and wrapped his beefy arms around her from behind.

"How are you doing, baby?"

"Fine. Have everything put away now."

"You're going to have to model some of that underwear for me sometime."

She felt her face heat up. "Maybe. Maybe not."

"Oh, you'll do it all right." He laughed. "I'll make sure of it. I'll throw all your old underwear away."

"You wouldn't dare." She glared at him.

"Oh, I would too."

"What are you two arguing about?" Brice asked as he walked into the room.

"Nothing," they both said together.

"For some reason I don't believe you, but I don't guess it's any of my business." Brice walked into the bathroom and closed the door.

Ronnie and Garrett exchanged glances. Neither one of them wanted Brice to leave, but they couldn't make him stay. Neither did they want him to stay out of guilt. Ronnie was afraid he would try to do that.

Brice emerged from the bathroom in a towel and said it was cold, if they wanted to risk it.

"I'd take a warm bath tomorrow if I were you. You can heat up the water. I probably would have done the same thing, but I was already in it by the time I realized it wasn't getting any warmer."

They all three climbed into bed, with Ronnie and Garrett snuggling together. Ronnie reached back to draw Brice into it. He seemed to hesitate then joined them.

* * * *

Brice wrapped his arms around her from behind and buried his nose against her neck. He loved the smell of her sweet skin.

Garrett rolled her over so that they both could reach her plump breasts. Brice sucked in a nipple and toyed with the nipple using his tongue. He reached between her legs and found her already wet.

"Her pussy is already wet with her juices, Garrett. She's begging for you to fuck her."

Garrett grinned and eased down the bed to taste her. Brice took over her other breast with his fingers. He molded it to his hand before concentrating on the nipple.

Without looking down, he knew Garrett was sucking on her hot cunt by the moans and whimpers coming from Ronnie's mouth. He sucked on her nipple, flattening it against the roof of his mouth. Then he nibbled on it until she grasped his head and held it still while she crammed her breast into his mouth.

"She's close, Brice. I want to be inside her when she comes," Garrett stood up next to the bed. "Baby, roll over and let me fuck you from behind. You can suck on Brice's cock like that."

"Yes, please. I'm so close. Don't make me wait." She quickly pulled from Brice's arms and rolled over to position her wet pussy so that Garrett could get to it.

Brice looked down the length of her back at her rounded ass and had to swallow down a groan. He wanted her so badly right then, he almost shoved Garrett aside. Instead, he knelt on the bed so that she had easy access to his throbbing cock.

When she began licking it, he tangled his fingers in her hair. He wanted to hold her head while she swallowed his dick. He wouldn't though. He didn't have the right to direct her loving. He was the outsider now. But for this one night, he was going to enjoy her sweet mouth.

She licked his balls then licked around the underside of his cockhead before licking the slit to retrieve the drop of pre-cum that had formed there. Then she swallowed his cock down as far as she could. On the way back up, she used her teeth lightly along the stalk.

He suppressed a moan when she began nibbling around the underside of his dick. She already knew his sensitive spots and exploited them without mercy.

The sight of her swallowing his cock with her lips stretched tight around it had his balls burning with his cum. He wouldn't last long. She grasped his dick around the base and began to take him deeper than ever before.

"Baby, I'm about to come. Swallow it all, Ronnie. Swallow it all."

He erupted down her throat. The force of it had him up on his toes as he throbbed in her mouth. When she had swallowed it all, she licked him until her own orgasm had her screaming.

That night, Brice shared in holding her while she slept. He lay there a long time just listening to her breath before he finally fell asleep.

* * * *

The next morning, Brice was gone. He'd left a note on the kitchen counter. He thanked them for being so good to him, but he needed to get on the road before the snow hit. He'd stop by when he was in the area. Reading between the lines, Ronnie knew he wouldn't do it. He was gone for good.

She wept off and on the rest of the day. Garrett hung around the house with her, trying to keep her mood lighter. Still, he was hurting, too. Brice hadn't even said a proper good-bye. Ronnie almost hated him for doing that to Garrett. She figured it was her fault and felt guilty.

"How about some deer meat for supper tonight? We can cook it with gravy and eat it with biscuits."

"Sounds good to me. You'll have to bring some up for me," Ronnie said.

She went out to milk the cow and feed the chickens before settling inside for the night. She couldn't help remembering how much Brice complained about milking the cow. He said it was like squeezing blood out of a turnip. She couldn't help but smile at that.

* * * *

Several weeks passed, and the snows came with a vengeance. They worked hard to keep the paths shoveled to the barn, the chickens and the pasture. They spent the rest of the day camped out in front of the fireplace.

Garrett teased her ear with his tongue and then sucked it in to his warm mouth. Ronnie giggled at the ticklish feelings he elicited when he played with her ears and her neck. He knew it turned her on, and she was obviously in a playful mood. He nibbled her jaw, then took her mouth in a deep kiss. His tongue sparred with hers before sucking hers deep into his mouth. He explored the roof of hers until they broke apart, breathless and laughing.

"I want you, Ronnie. I want to fuck you deep and hard. Can you handle that?"

"Oh, I can handle anything you give me."

"On your hands and knees."

Ronnie laughed and pulled off her jeans. They'd already pulled their boots off when they came in the house. She slipped out of her panties, the frilly ones, and got on her hands and knees in front of the fire.

Garrett tested her readiness with his fingers. He fucked her with them until he was satisfied she was wet enough to handle him. He lined his dick up with her slit and pushed in until he met resistance. Then he pulled out and shoved it in further. Finally, on the third try, he managed to lodge himself all the way against her cervix. He held still to let her adjust to him. After a few seconds, he began tunneling in and out of her, over and over. She moaned, knowing it turned him on for her to do it. It turned her on to hear him grunting as he fucked her hard and deep. Each time he bumped her cervix, she squeezed him with her cunt muscles. It had just an edge of pain to it that burned her up inside.

In this position, he was able to reach around and play with her breasts and her clit. Occasionally, he'd spank her as he grew closer to his climax. It soon had her in tears, but pushing back hard against him. She liked the bite of pain with the heat and thrill of her climax. He always made sure she climaxed.

This time, he gathered some of her juices creaming down her leg and rubbed them in her back hole. She stiffened, and he immediately stopped to assure her it was okay.

"Push back against my thumb, baby. I promise it will feel so good once I'm inside you."

She swallowed around the lump in her throat and pushed back as he pushed inward. It popped through the ring of resistance, and he let her get used to his thumb being inside her before he began to pull out and push back in, in time with his thrusting his cock inside of her cunt. Nerve endings woke inside her that she'd never known existed before now. She began to thrust back against him as he tunneled in and out of her.

The slight burn turned into something altogether different. She trembled at the intensity of her orgasm rolling her way. She slammed back as he pushed forward. He reached around her and fingered her clit, sending her spiraling into her climax. She called out his name, clamping down on his dick. Then she felt his cum pouring into her, and she went off again in tiny sparks.

When he pulled out of her, she whimpered. The loss was that much greater now that he pulled out of her back hole as well. He left her lying prone on the rug to wash up in the bathroom. The next thing she felt was a washcloth cleaning between her legs and around her ass.

He pulled her down to the soft rug in front of the fireplace and hugged her. His warm breath on the back of her neck was one of the most comforting feelings in the world. She snuggled into him and was nearly asleep when he eased from her and picked her up.

"What are you doing?" she mumbled sleepily.

"Putting you on the couch while I go tend to the animals."

"Oh, I almost forgot. I better go see to the cow. She needs milking. You can't do it. Your hands are too big." She laughed and struggled to her feet.

"I'm sorry, baby. I had hoped you could sleep some." Garrett helped her dress.

They put on coats, gloves, scarves, and hats, and opened the kitchen door to over a foot of fresh snow.

"This is going to take a little bit longer than I thought," Garrett said with a sigh.

They each grabbed their snow shovels and scooped the snow away as they headed for the barn and the chicken coop.

Instead of stopping at the coop to feed the chickens, Garrett continued shoveling to the barn for her. Then he headed for the pasture. Ronnie opened the barn door against the blowing wind and closed it again. It wasn't quite as cold inside as it was outside, thanks to there being no wind. She sat down on the stool and proceeded to milk the cow. She had begun to produce a full bucket again, and this made her think of Brice and his inability to get more than a half a bucket from the poor cow.

She carted the milk to the house and sat it in the cool kitchen with a towel over the top. Back outside, she headed to the chicken coop. She opened the door, and several of the hens flew out only to fly right back in as she began to add feed to their pens. She scattered some on the floor as well. They didn't squabble much when she closed the door and scrambled to the pasture to see if Garrett needed any help with the hay.

He was forking some out into the hay feeder. He seemed to be almost finished, but she waited on him anyway. They walked hand in hand back to the house, carrying their shovels. Once inside the house, they stripped out of their outer garments, leaving her boots at the back door. Garrett finished pulling off his boots and set them next to hers. She stared at them, thinking how right they looked next to each other. But a third pair was missing.

She struggled to put that out of her mind. She didn't want Garrett thinking she wasn't happy with him, because she was. She just missed Brice.

* * * *

Garrett crawled out of bed one morning to find that the sun was shining and the snow had begun to melt. He didn't think about the mess it would make as it melted until he slipped in the mud. He had been checking the fences out in the pasture. He landed on his ass and cursed as he got up. He was in a foul mood when he returned to the house to change out of his wet clothes.

He met Ronnie coming back out from putting away the eggs. She narrowed her eyebrows.

"What in the world happened to you?"

"Slipped in the fucking mud," he snapped at her.

She quickly closed her mouth at his look. He could tell that she thought it was funny. She quickly turned around and headed back to the house.

"Strip off down here, Garrett, so I can put them in the tub to soak."

He grumbled the entire time he undressed. He was wet and muddy down to his thermals, and cold as well. He watched her put a bucket of water on the stove to heat up.

"Run the tub half-full, and I'll bring up some warm water for you."

"No, you go run the bath. I'll bring up the bucket when it gets warm. You're not carrying a full bucket up the damn stairs." He sighed and stomped toward the living room, where he could stand in front of the fire until it was ready.

When he took the water upstairs, she had everything out for him. He poured the scalding water into the tub, then stirred the water until it was a pleasant, warm temperature, and stepped in. He eased down into the tub and sighed. When he picked up the cloth to bathe, Ronnie took it away from him and began to soap it up.

"I'll bathe you. You just relax and enjoy the warm water."

She cleansed him from head to toe. When he would have gotten out of the water, she lathered up her hand and wrapped it around his cock. It went from half-mast to attention in no time at all under her careful ministrations. He groaned as she began a slow, teasing rhythm. He reached around her hand and tightened her grip around him.

"You won't hurt me. Just like that."

She squeezed him harder and began to slide her hand up and down the thick stalk of his dick. She twisted her hand slightly when she did, and he moaned. His cock grew harder as she pulled on it over and over. Then she reached into the water and located his balls. They were already tight and boiling with his cum. She gently ran them around in her hand as she pulled and tugged on his dick. When he was close, his balls drew up, and she redoubled her efforts at jacking him off. He couldn't believe she was actually doing it. It felt so much different when she did it than when he did.

She ran her hand over the top of his cock and ran her thumb around the slit before squeezing her way down his dick again. He shivered, and it wasn't the cooling water. Suddenly, he felt the burn down his spine as his cum shot from his balls out of his cock. She continued to pull on him, slowing down when he stopped shooting cum. She smiled at him and brought her hand covered in his cum to her mouth. She slowly licked it all off.

"Fuck, baby. That was so good."

"I wanted to make you feel better. Did it work?"

"Better than anything." He rinsed off and climbed out of the tub.

"Let's get you dried off and in some dry clothes before you get sick. I don't know what I'd do without you, Garrett." She snuggled up against his nude body and whispered, "I love you, Garrett." His heart stuttered at the quiet admission. He squeezed her tight.

"I love you, Ronnie." He'd never thought to say the words before, though he'd known that he loved her for well over a month now.

"I've got to dress and get back out there and finish feeding the cows."

"Try not to fall again," she teased him.

He smiled. "Not if I can help it. That was a cold wake up. I didn't realize that the snow had melted so fast."

"Actually, it melts faster in the pasture because of the added heat of the cows. I doubt you would have slipped anywhere else in the yard yet. I dread this part of winter. Everything starts to thaw, and you end up with a great big muddy mess. It's hell on the floors if you don't remember to take off your boots."

Once he had clothes on again, Garrett grabbed Ronnie around the waist and tangled his fingers up in her long hair. He pulled her up to meet his kiss. He let her take the lead and he followed. It was a very sensuous kiss. She let him know in it that she truly did love him.

This time, when he went out, he was careful to walk on dryer patches and hold on to the fence line. One of the cows came up and sniffed him as he reached back for some hay to throw over in their pile to be eaten.

"Scoot back, cow. I don't want you to slide and fall on me. I might never get up again." He swatted the cow on the flanks and watched it amble away toward the hay. He laughed they seemed to maneuver in the muddy pasture without a problem. He shook his head and completed that round of chores and headed for the barn to feed the milking cow and horses.

Over and over again his mind went back to her hand wrapped around his dick and her other hand playing with his balls. It had felt so damn good. He'd never thought to ask her to do that before. He hoped it would become something they did on a semi-regular basis. He sure as hell wouldn't complain. He would never push anything on her, but he also wanted in her sweet ass. He was slowly preparing her. He'd go a little further tonight. The idea soon had his cock standing up at attention pushing on the zipper of his jeans very uncomfortably.

Chapter Ten

Winter turned into spring and the real work around the farm began. Garrett was amazed that Ronnie had been able to do so much on her own. Then, you did what you had to do to survive. It would be a little easier on her this year, he vowed. For one thing, he took over the plowing. He broke up new ground along with the old ground so that the garden was almost double in size.

Then he hilled it up and left it for her to plant it as she wanted to. She told him he would need to plow between the rows for several weeks until the vegetables grew enough that they didn't need the extra aeration to grow larger. She planted everything from butter beans to squash. She also added lots of tomatoes.

"I can them for sauces to add to chili, spaghetti, lasagna, and soups."

Garrett plowed up land for hay. They needed to grow as much of their own hay as possible. It would cut down on needing to barter for more. She showed him how to sow the seeds then left him to finish. He was amazed at just how much he didn't know. She seemed to know everything about living off the earth.

Once all the planting had taken place, they had newborn calves to see to. They spent several nights out in the barn helping pull the calves free of their moms. All in all, she ended up with three new calves. She was excited. She said they were cute little things, all wobbly on their legs. He thought she was the cute one, with her hair all mussed and the delighted expression on her face. He couldn't help loving her. She meant more to him than anything. He only wished Brice was there to share in it.

"What are you thinking about? You look so sad."

"Sorry, baby. Just thinking. Let's go clean up. It's nearly dark out now."

"You miss him, don't you?" she finally said when they were inside.

"Yeah, I do. We were together for nearly ten years." Garrett washed up in the utility sink after removing his boots.

"He'll come back. It may not be this year, but he'll be back."

"Enough about him, let's start supper. I'm starved." He picked her up and swung her around in his arms.

"You're always hungry. I hope we planted enough vegetables, or we just might starve," she teased.

"You've been eating like a horse, too, with all the work we've been doing," he reminded her.

She stuck her tongue out at him and started pulling together their supper.

Once they'd finished washing up, they stripped down to nothing and climbed into the shower for a lukewarm bath. The cooler water felt good on their feverish skin. He helped her wash, then let her return the favor for him. When she got down on her knees, he was reminded again how fortunate he was to have found someone like Ronnie.

She wrapped her hands around his cock and licked him from top to bottom before surrounding the mushroom cap and sucking hard enough to roll his eyes back in his head. When she dipped her tongue into the slit, he hissed out a breath and wound her hair in his hands to keep it out of her face. She tongued the underside of his cock, then sucked the skin in just enough to curl his toes. When she finally sucked him down her throat, he was already close to shooting off.

Ronnie rolled his balls with one hand as she sucked her way down over and over again. When she raked his balls with her nails and his dick with her teeth, he felt lightening hit down his spine and spread out until his balls drew up and he filled her throat with his cum. She continued sucking then licked him until he was clean. He groaned as he fought to catch his breath. It seemed like each time was better than the last time. She knew exactly what he needed to come, and she teased and tormented him until he did.

"Baby, you don't know how good that felt. Lean back against the tile, I want to eat that pussy of yours. I know it will be nice and wet for me. You're always wet for me."

Ronnie smiled up at him and stood up with his help. Then she leaned back against the cool tile as Garrett slipped to his knees to nuzzle her belly with his mouth. He loved her rounded belly and the way she was ticklish at the juncture of her thighs. He teased her with his tongue then spread her pussy lips wide so he could delve right into her wet cunt.

She moaned when he licked over her clit. He didn't linger there, though. That was for later. First, he wanted her hot and needy before he let her come. He pushed two fingers inside of her sweet pussy and fucked her as he licked her slit from top to bottom. He curled his tongue to get as much of her juices as he could. She tasted like warm honey, and he couldn't get enough of her.

"God, Ronnie, you have the best taste in the world. I could make a meal off of you, and come back for seconds."

"I need more, Garrett. Please, I can't stand it. Harder."

He grinned and pumped harder with his fingers then added a third finger. She hissed out a *yes* as he shoved them in and out of her. He continued to lick and suck at her pussy lips. When she was trying to ram down on his fingers, he curled them up and stroked her sweet spot deep inside. She came up on her toes and grabbed his head trying to push him toward her clit.

Instead, he nipped her cunt with gentle teeth and continued to fuck her with his hands, then curl around and stroke that special spot. Finally, he took pity on her whimpering and crying out for more and sucked her clit between his teeth and nipped it. She exploded around him. He couldn't lick fast enough to suck down all her cunt juices. He felt them bathe his face.

When she'd calmed down enough that he could let her go without fear of her falling, he stood up and rinsed his face in the shower. He handed her the bath cloth to clean up again.

"You always make me fly, Garrett."

"I love it when you come all over my face. I know I've made you feel good."

They climbed out of the shower and dried off, then headed to bed. It was too hot to do much of anything but hold hands. They slept without a sheet and without clothes to try and stay cool. They had started leaving the windows open at night to catch any breeze that blew up.

Garrett was used to the heat, having worked out in it while out scavenging, but he wasn't so sure that Ronnie did well in it. She tended not to want to eat much when she was hot. He could tell she'd lost some weight, and it worried him.

Finally, he drifted off to thoughts of how it could have been with Brice living with them.

* * * *

Several weeks passed, and the garden needed weeding and watering on a regular basis. They tended to get brief showers, but not really enough to soak the ground well. He hauled water to the hay field, though Ronnie said she had never done it before, and it did all right. He wanted to make as much hay as possible. She used the hoses to water the garden. He was glad he'd remembered to get them for her when he and Brice had gone to Sky Line. She had to carry water the last few years. Now she just turned it on and laid it in the center aisles for a couple of hours each evening.

"Let's sleep downstairs tonight. It's cooler down here than up in the bedroom." Ronnie handed him a glass of tea, then poured one for herself.

"Sounds like a good idea to me, too. We can use that blow-up bed I brought back, so we'll be fairly comfortable."

"I'll get a sheet so we aren't sticking to the plastic. Do you have to blow it up by mouth?" she asked.

"No, it has a foot pump." He grabbed her arm when she turned to go upstairs, and planted a kiss on her mouth.

"What was that for?" she asked with a grin.

"Just because."

She giggled and wrapped her arms around him even though they were both sticky and dirty. They'd take a shower together later, and then relax to sleep.

Not long after he had the bed blown up and they had spread the sheet over the bed, they took a cool shower and walked back downstairs nude to settle down for the night. Garrett looked at his watch. It was only nine, but they tended to get up early to beat as much of the heat as possible.

The sound of a vehicle pulling up the drive had them both scrambling to pull on the clothes they kept near them when they slept nude. A door shut outside and then there were footsteps on the front porch.

"Go upstairs and stay there until I call for you."

"You might need me, Garrett," she argued.

"Don't argue with me about this. Go upstairs now, Ronnie," he said in a stern voice.

She nodded and ran up the stairs. He waited until she was out of sight and then crossed to the door to wait for a knock. When it came, it was more of a pounding than a knock. He called through the door.

"Who is it?"

"It's Brice, man. Let me the fuck in."

Garrett quickly unlocked the locks on the door and let his friend in. As soon as the other man crossed the threshold, he pulled him into a bear hug.

"How the hell are you, Brice?"

"Okay, missing the two of you. Do you think Ronnie would let me move back?"

"I don't know. You'll have to take that up with her. You know I want you back, but she was really hurt that you left."

Brice winced and nodded. "I thought it was for the best at the time, but I miss her so much. She completed me. Without her all these months, I've been surviving instead of living."

"Let me call her down. I sent her upstairs because we didn't know who it could be."

"Sorry I scared you. I sure didn't mean to. I probably should have waited until daylight to show up, but I was in such a hurry to get back, I didn't stop to think."

Garrett closed the door and relocked the locks before ushering Brice further into the living room.

"Sleeping down here now?"

"It's hot upstairs, so we thought we'd try this tonight. It's a little cooler down here." Garrett crossed to the stairs and called up for Ronnie to come down.

She walked down the stairs with a disgruntled expression on her face but it soon brightened when she saw Brice. Then she closed down, and her expression turned neutral.

"Hi, Brice. How are you?"

"Missing you and Garrett. Can I have a hug, baby?" he asked in a quiet voice.

"Are you leaving again?"

"Depends on if you'll have me back or not."

Garrett watched her seem to think on it for a few seconds. Then she grinned and ran and jumped in Brice's arms.

"You promise? You're back for good? No more slipping off?"

"No more slipping off. I'm back for good. I was miserable without you two. Nothing meant anything without you two to share it with."

"There's a lot of work involved," Ronnie warned him.

"With three of us it should be a bit easier than with just two."

"I've missed you so much, Brice. It hurt when you left."

"I know, baby. I'm really sorry." He drew in a deep breath and let it out. "I'm going to be harder to live with than Garrett is. He pretty much lets you do as you want. I won't be that way."

She smirked and raked her nails down his pant leg over his cock. "I think I can handle you."

Brice swallowed and Garrett laughed at his friend's discomfort. She would put him through his paces before she let him back into her heart. She'd had enough heartache. But things were looking up and soon would be back to normal.

"Might as well get naked and make yourself at home. We are very informal here in the summer because it *is* so freaking hot," Garrett told him.

"Is there going to be room on that bed for the three of us?" he asked, eyeing the contraption.

"If not, you can sleep on the couch," Ronnie was quick to point out.

* * * *

Brice couldn't believe he was back. He hoped he would be able to call it home soon. Right now, he felt as if he was on probation, and maybe he was. Ronnie wasn't going to welcome him back with open arms like Garrett did. He'd hurt her, and she hadn't forgotten it. He only hoped she would forgive him sometime in the future.

He climbed the stairs and took a cold shower. He was tempted to jack off so he wouldn't be so obvious about his lust for Ronnie, but decided she needed to know how badly he wanted her. He would just have to suffer the night with a stiff dick. It wasn't like he hadn't been doing it for months now.

When he made it back downstairs, they were already on the blow-up mattress curled up against each other. He climbed on and instantly felt uncomfortable, since he wasn't touching her. He started to get up and get on the couch, but she reached out and took his hand.

"It's really too hot to sleep close to each other. We're going to spread out too in a minute. Hold my hand until we go to sleep, Brice."

He didn't hesitate but took her hand and brought it to his lips, then settled it between them. A few minutes later, she and Garrett spread out some, and once again, they all were together.

"I hope you know that cow-milking duty is yours for the week," Ronnie warned him.

He groaned then laughed. "Poor cow. I hope you realize it's her you're punishing."

"She'll get over it." Ronnie laughed. "Besides, you need to keep up your skills. You never know when I might not be able to do it for a day or two."

"What have you been doing with yourself, Brice?" Garrett asked with a yawn.

"Same thing we used to do, but on my own. Barter Town is even worse than it used to be. Lots of under-the-table stuff going on there now. They are dealing more and more with the black-market slave trade. They even have auctions in the open."

"Fuck, the world isn't screwed up enough, we have to have women treated like cattle." Garrett huffed out a breath.

"It gets worse. They've started a sort of gang of sorts to administer justice to anyone caught helping a female escape their man or men. They're whipping them, Garrett. I couldn't stand it, I had to leave."

Ronnie stilled. "What if Carl shows up and tells them I ran away from him? Oh, God, what's going to happen to me?"

"Shhh, Ronnie. Nothing is going to happen to you. You're with us, and we won't let it." Garrett pulled her back in his arms.

The fact that Garrett had included him as being there to help protect her made him feel good inside. He would do anything and everything to make sure nothing happened to her.

"I doubt Carl will show up out here looking for you. More than likely after all this time he's forgotten all about you, Ronnie."

"I hope so. I'm scared, Garrett. Brice, how do they find out about the women?"

"The man or men turn them in as runaways and the gang searches for them. They charge them with being a runaway and administer the whipping right then and there."

"So they're judge and jury," Garrett commented.

"Well, don't worry about it, Ronnie. Carl won't find you here. I have to doubt he would travel all the way out here." Brice squeezed her hand and brought it to his lips again. This time he gave her palm a kiss. "I'll protect you with my life, Ronnie."

"Please don't let it come down to that. I don't want to lose either one of you." She licked her lips and shuddered.

"I think it's time to get some sleep. Dawn comes early, and we want to take advantage of all the cooler morning hours that we can." Garrett leaned over to the light and doused it.

Brice felt the complete darkness settle over him like a cloak. He was used to the stars and moon shedding their light on him when it wasn't raining. Still, some of the moon's light sifted through the curtains and left a sliver of light to knife through the room to the staircase.

The more he thought about it, the more he was sure he'd made the right decision to come home. Now that he'd been reminded that Ronnie had run away from a man, the more worried he became. What if Carl showed up and accused her of running away? What could they do against a gang of men? He would have to discuss it with Garrett once Ronnie wasn't around. He didn't want her to worry more than she already was.

He squeezed her hand and went to sleep.

Chapter Eleven

Brice rose early the next morning while it was still dark outside. He tried to get up off the mattress without waking the others but didn't manage to do it. First Ronnie woke up stretching. Then Garrett was rolling out of bed as well.

"Sorry, didn't mean to wake you. It's hard to get off that damn thing without making waves." He chuckled.

"That's all right. We usually are up about this time anyway. I'll get the eggs and you get the milk," she teased.

He watched her dress even as he climbed back into his old clothes. She wore jeans and the frilly underwear they'd gotten her back in Sky Line. She didn't bother with a bra but put on a work shirt. She handed him the bucket, and she took the basket. They walked outside together and walked side by side until they reached the chicken coop. Then she unlatched the door and opened it for the chickens to spread out around the yard. She threw out some feed and added a few piles here and there. Then she started egg searching.

Brice realized he'd been standing there for nearly five minutes watching her when he should have been milking the damn cow. He carried the stool over and sat down. Then he and the cow had a talk, and he started milking. He realized it was like riding a bike. You never really forget how to do it. It all came back to him fairly quickly. Before long, he had a half bucket of milk. He carried it into the house and went ahead and strained it for Ronnie. Then he set it down in the cellar where it was cooler. It would spoil soon, so he poured a glass and drank it.

When he walked back outside it was to find Garrett waiting on him. "We're going to check the fences today. We have three new calves, so we want to be sure everything is tight."

"Sounds good. I'll help any way I can."

Brice walked the fence line with Garrett and helped repair a broken wire, then continued on their path.

"Garrett, I'm worried about this Carl person coming after Ronnie. The gang is more serious than I was letting on. They are taking cases. If someone lost a woman, they describe her or produce a picture of her, and the gang is looking for them."

"Fuck, that's all we need. Is there any way to find out who they might be looking for at any given time?"

"Not that I've figured out. All we can do is be on the watch out for them or this Carl person."

"Hell, one of us needs to be close to the house at all times," Garrett said.

"Teach me everything you can, and I'll work the fields while you watch after her." Brice wanted to be the one to care for her, but knew he wasn't all the way back into her good graces yet."

"No, we take turns."

"If you're sure. I'm happy to do whatever you need me to."

"All I care about is taking care of Ronnie. Whatever it takes."

"Let's get back to the house and work out what all needs doing and divide it up so that one of us is always near her and the house." Garrett led the way.

Brice had to walk fast to keep up with the big man. He was obviously in a hurry. Brice didn't fault him for wanting to get back to her. He did, too. He had a bad feeling that Carl was going to end up being a problem.

"Hey, Ronnie! Where are you?" Garrett called out as they walked into the yard.

"In the garden. Is something wrong?" She came running out.

"Nope, just wondering where you were. We've finished the pasture for the day. Getting awfully hot out here. You ready to go in until it cools off some?"

"In a few minutes. I'm almost finished picking butter beans. We'll have them for supper tonight." She turned around and walked back into the garden.

"I'll go keep her company," Brice offered.

"Sounds like a good idea. You can try and get back in her good graces," Garrett said with a chuckle.

Brice followed Ronnie back into the middle of the garden where she was pulling the beans off the vine and dropping them into a bucket.

"Need some help?" he asked.

"Naw, I don't have much more to go. Plus, you might not pick the right ones." She smirked at him.

"You're probably right." He laughed with her.

"Why did you come back, Brice?"

"I missed you and Garrett. I realized that my home is here with you, if you'll have me back."

"You're always welcome here, Brice. I just need to know if you plan to stay or not. I can't wonder from day to day if you're going to leave again." She continued picking beans.

"I'm not going anywhere. I care for you very much. I don't know. Maybe it's even more than that. I just know that my life was empty without you in it."

"I guess we have to take it one day at a time for now."

"That's all I can ask for." He picked up the bucket when she stood up.

"I want to make a detour by the tomatoes to see if there are any ripe yet. I've wanted a tomato sandwich for days now."

"After you. I don't know where they are." He followed her around to the outside where there were two rows of tomato plants. She chose several that were ripe or nearly ripe and added them to his bucket.

"Now for the okra." She walked up to the stalks and cut off a handful and tossed them in the bucket as well. "I guess that's it for today."

"You look exhausted, Ronnie. Why don't you take a cool shower and then take a nap?"

"That sounds like heaven."

"Will you let me bathe you?" He hurried on when she looked ready to say no. "Just bathe you, nothing more."

She seemed to think about it as she separated the vegetables on the cabinet. She bit her lower lip and nodded her head.

He let out a breath he hadn't realized he'd been holding.

She climbed the stairs to the bathroom with him right behind her. He waited as she gathered her bath supplies and turned on the water, then he helped her undress. Once she was nude, she helped him undress, and they both stepped into the shower together.

He'd forgotten how perfect her body was, rounded, heavy breasts with a slightly rounded belly and a plump ass. He loved looking at her. He soaped up a cloth and began bathing her from neck to toes. He paid special attention to her breasts, but she didn't complain or pull away. He became a bit bolder and spread her legs slightly so he could clean her pussy. He soaped her up then rinsed her before probing her sweet cunt with his fingers. She closed her eyes and leaned her head back.

Brice took it as an invitation to explore more. He bent down and sucked her nipple into his mouth while his fingers explored her wet pussy. He slowly pumped two fingers in and out of her over and over while licking and sucking her nipple, then all of her breast he could fit into his mouth.

When he pulled back and nipped at it, she grabbed his head and directed it to the other breast. He repeated the process on this one, and then alternated as his fingers fucked her sweet cunt. When he thumbed her clit, she called out his name and went up on her tiptoes. He slowly brought her down then pulled her in for a kiss.

"We better clean you up again and dry you off."

"That was wonderful, Brice. Thank you."

"I loved it as much as you did. You're so beautiful when you come."

After he'd rinsed her off, he helped her dry off. Garrett walked in the bedroom as they were walking out of the bathroom.

"So not fair. I wanted to take a shower, too."

"You can take one. It'll just be by yourself." Ronnie chuckled and swatted him on the ass.

"He made you come, didn't he?" Garrett said.

"Yes, but I didn't have sex with her. Don't be angry with her, Garrett."

"I'm not angry, just jealous. I wanted to watch her come."

"She's beautiful when she comes, isn't she," Brice said.

"Yeah."

"Come here, Ronnie. I want a taste of you." Garrett curled his finger at her.

She backed away with a grin on her face. "You'll have to catch me first."

She ran over to the bed and got on it. He ran around one side and Brice ran around to the other. They both jumped on the bed to tackle her but missed when she squeezed past them to the end of the bed and hurried down the stairs.

"Don't you dare fall down those stairs," Garrett called after her.

She ran into the living room and stood behind the couch, ready to run again. Only thing was, Brice was on one side and Garrett on the other. Brice was thoroughly enjoying himself. They closed in on her and she attempted to climb over the couch. This time, Garrett caught her and hauled her over his shoulder. He swatted her ass with two quick swats.

"Hey!" she yelped.

"Teach you to run from me." He swatted her two more times, then stuck his fingers between her legs and grinned. He pulled them out and sucked her fresh cream from his fingers.

"Want to taste her, Brice?" He turned Ronnie's ass toward Brice.

Brice thought he was in heaven as he dipped his fingers into her sweet, wet pussy. He sucked her juices from his fingers and closed his eyes in ecstasy.

"She tastes like a dream." Brice licked his lips.

"I'm going to fuck this sweet ass of hers one day, but she's not ready yet." He slapped her ass one more time, then let her slide to the ground where she glared at him.

"You keep spanking me and you'll never get in my ass, mister." She rubbed her ass with her hands.

"I think I'll fuck that delectable pussy instead. Get on your hands and knees, Ronnie. I want you to suck Brice's cock while I'm fucking you."

"Garrett, she doesn't have to. It's too early." Brice tried to figure out how to say no without upsetting Ronnie into thinking he didn't want her. He didn't want her to have to do something if she didn't want to.

"Ronnie?" Garrett asked.

"I want to suck your cock, Brice. You feel different in my mouth than Garrett does. I missed you." She got down on her hands and knees on the floor rug and licked her lips. Then she looked over her shoulder at where Garrett was undressing.

Brice didn't need a second urging. He sat on the edge of the couch so that he was at the perfect height for her to take his dick in her mouth. She leaned in and licked his balls first, then ran her tongue up and down his cock as he held her hair back from her face. When she nibbled underneath the head of his cock, he nearly came off the couch. It felt so damn good. She sucked around the crown then licked the head like a lollipop.

Garrett was standing behind her now. He knelt and lined up his cock with her slit before shoving it in as far as he could go. This shoved her mouth down his cock until she nearly gagged, but instead of pulling off of him, she swallowed around him making him shout out.

"Fuck!"

"She had you, man. Just wait, you'll be curling your toes soon."

Then he began making shallow thrusts until he was obviously in as far as he could go. His constant pushes had her sucking his cock down in time with Garrett fucking her. Then she used his timing to suck Brice's cock down over and over. The faster he moved, the faster she swallowed him down. She wrapped one hand around his dick to counter her movements. Ronnie looked up at him as she went down on him again. Her eyes rolled up to meet his and went straight to his heart. He knew in that instant that he truly loved her. He'd loved her since they'd first been together. He had fought it all this time. He was all out of fighting now. He just wanted to love her.

Brice was doing a number on her, thrusting hard and fast. She was thrusting back against him as fast as she could while keeping Brice's cock in her mouth. Finally she pulled back from his cock as Garrett reached around and fiddled with her clit until she was screaming and almost convulsing in her climax. As soon as he had finished with her, Brice shoved his cock back into her mouth. He knew she was having trouble breathing, so he didn't shove it down her throat. Instead, he held her head still and shallowly face fucked her until he felt his cum boiling in his balls. He was about to come and wanted to wait a little longer. He fought it hard, but when she came back up him with her teeth, he lost it and shot all his cum deep in her mouth and throat. She swallowed it all and licked him clean.

He fell back against the back of the couch, totally exhausted. Between the walking and workout in the heat, and then the shower and now the blow job, he was wasted. He crawled off the couch after several long seconds and curled up on the mattress. Ronnie and Garrett laughed as soon as they were able to catch their breath.

"What's so fucking funny?" Brice grumbled.

"You are. You're totally exhausted. You've got to build up some stamina," Garrett told him.

"Don't worry. I'll be in better shape soon enough working in this place. It has to have been made for at least six kids. There are six bedrooms."

"True, but they have one as a parlor or something, and one as an office. You've never really been all the way through it. It does need a lot of work." She shrugged. "Right now, it takes everything we have to keep the farm up."

"Well, I'm here to help now. Between the three of us, we'll get more done and with less suffering," Brice promised.

"Okay you two. Settle down and let's get a nap. It will be time to get back out there in another few hours."

Brice smiled, finally feeling a little more like he belonged again.

* * * *

Two days later, they decided they were going to have to go to Sky Line for more supplies. This time, they decided that Brice would stay with Ronnie. Garrett would go since he knew what parts he was looking for, for the tractor. Ronnie complained about needing a babysitter.

"Baby, we don't want to take a chance of leaving you here alone. Remember last time," Garrett reminded her.

"I know. It just seems so stupid that I have to worry about it at all." Ronnie looked over at Brice. "It wouldn't matter if it were Garrett staying and you going, Brice. I would still feel the same way."

"I know, Ronnie."

"Well, since you're going, I need some things." She pulled out a pad and pencil and began making a list.

Garrett rolled his eyes and she glared at him. Brice grinned at him. Ronnie glared at him as well.

She really wanted to go with them, but they didn't want her exposed to the wolves. They told her they couldn't watch out for her and the wolves at the same time. She sighed and finished her list. She handed it to Garrett, warning him not to lose it.

"I really need those canning supplies, Garrett, so I can put up our excess vegetables."

"I'll find some for you, baby." He kissed her. "I'll leave early in the morning."

They finished up the evening chores in record time. All three of them showered together, washing each other's backs, and both men paid close attention to Ronnie's breasts.

Ronnie licked across Garrett's wet chest from nipple to nipple. Then she slowly sank to her knees as she licked her way down to his throbbing cock. He grinned down at her when she looked up. She knew he loved for her to suck his dick.

"Baby, I want to see Brice fuck your wet pussy. Get up and bend over for him, Ronnie." Garrett pulled her to her feet. "You can suck my cock like this."

Ronnie bent over and took Garrett's thick dick in her mouth as she presented her ass to Brice. She felt him run his cock up and down in her pussy juices before pushing into her cunt. His thick dick stretched her deliciously.

"Oh, God. Please, Brice. I need more." She couldn't stand him teasing her.

"I don't want to hurt you, baby."

"You won't hurt her, Brice. She likes it fast and hard." Garrett groaned when Ronnie sucked his cock into her mouth.

Brice thrust harder into her wet pussy until he managed to make it all the way inside. Then he held himself there until Ronnie couldn't take it anymore. She thrust back against him in hopes he would get the message that she needed him to move.

She sucked and licked on Garrett, trying to concentrate on his pleasure in an effort to prolong her own. She knew if she dwelt on how good Brice's cock felt inside of her, she would come too soon. She wanted it to last. This was the first time Brice had fucked her.

"That's it, baby. Swallow around me like that. Fuck, that feels good." Garrett ran a hand through her hair, then scraped his nails against her scalp.

Brice began to move inside of her in earnest now. He thrust hard, pulling almost all the way out each time. His hands gripped her hips, pulling her back on his rigid dick over and over again. He bumped against her cervix with each thrust.

Ronnie began to lose her rhythm with Garrett as a burning began low in her spine. It curled through her cunt and centered in her clit. She wasn't going to last much longer. It rushed toward her like a locomotive over railroad tracks. She reached for it, wanting to experience it with Brice.

"I'm going to come, Brice. Please, more," she managed to get out.

He took her at her word and began to pound into her cunt with more force. She held on tightly to Garrett for balance. She would finish him afterwards but couldn't suck on him with Brice tunneling in and out of her pussy like a mad man.

Her orgasm hit her like an explosion. It blew through her and over her until she was screaming Brice's name. She felt it the instant he erupted inside of her. Hot cum bathed her cunt as he came, calling out her name.

As soon as she had recovered enough to think, she took Garrett's still-hard dick into her mouth and swallowed around him over and over until he spilled his cum into her mouth. She swallowed, then licked him clean.

She loved how they took care of her afterward. Brice cleaned her up and then Garrett dried her off. Garrett carried her downstairs to the makeshift bed on the floor, and all three of them climbed on to fall asleep almost immediately.

When Garrett got up early the next morning to go, Ronnie woke up and went with him upstairs to dress.

"Please be careful, Garrett. I hate for you to go alone. I'll worry about you until you get back home."

"I'll be fine. You keep close to Brice for me. No wandering off like you're prone to do when you're not paying attention."

"I'll be good," she teased.

"See that you are, or I'll spank that sweet ass of yours."

"Promises, promises."

"Okay, I have your list in my pocket. You need to lay back down for another hour or so."

"I will once I see you out." She followed him downstairs and they tiptoed past Brice, who was snoring softly.

Garrett opened the door then turned back to Ronnie to kiss her. She pulled him down for a deeper kiss. She slid her tongue along his, and he nipped at it before sucking it into his mouth and teasing it. When they broke apart, she was breathing hard.

"I love you, Garrett," she whispered as he let go of her and headed for the truck. She watched him get in then quietly closed the door so the truck noise wouldn't wake Brice up.

She was wide awake now. She couldn't go back to sleep, so she pulled on her T-shirt and padded into the kitchen to make coffee. It wasn't long before Brice shuffled in wearing only his jeans. He rubbed his eyes and headed straight to the coffee.

"Morning to you, too, Brice," Ronnie teased.

"Sorry, Ronnie. Morning." He poured a cup from the strained coffee and took a tentative sip before settling down at the kitchen table.

"He get off okay?"

"Yeah. I'll worry about him till he gets back safely."

"I know. I will, too." He took another sip of coffee. "So, do you want me to take care of milking the cow this morning?"

"No, I'll do that. You feed the cows and whatever else you do out there. I'll tend to the garden."

"Do you have a gun, Ronnie?" he asked her.

"We have a couple of guns, why?"

"If you have a handgun, I think you need to carry it with you in the pocket of an apron. I know that will be something extra to carry around, but you might need it. If you need help, you can fire it up in the air, and I'll come running."

"I guess so. I don't much like them." Ronnie shrugged.

"Go get it and I'll check it over."

Ronnie ran up the stairs and pulled out the handgun from the dresser drawer. It wasn't a large one by any means, but it would serve its purpose, she supposed. When she handed it to Brice, he nodded.

"This should fit well in your pocket and your hand."

"I'd rather not have to carry it, Brice. I don't like handguns. They're dangerous."

"Not any more so than that shotgun of yours."

"Okay. But I think this is overkill. Nothing is going to happen." She slipped the gun in an apron pocket. She'd wear it to do the chores. It would be a bit hotter, but she would deal with it.

She pulled it on and grabbed her basket and bucket. "I'm going to go ahead and start chores."

"Wait and let me get my boots on, too. I'll go with you."

"Don't you think you're taking this a bit too seriously?" She really didn't want him tagging along behind her so that she ran over him when she turned around.

"Nope, I promised Garrett I wouldn't let you out of my sight. I plan on keeping that promise."

"Then how are you going to feed the cows?" she asked with a smirk.

"When you've finished your chores, you'll come with me to feed the cows, and then I'll go with you to work in the garden. If you tell me what to do in the garden, I can help, and we will finish before it gets too hot. We'll want to rest up until Garrett gets back, so we can help him unload." Brice stood up and walked over to the utility room and pulled on his boots.

Ronnie did the same thing and grabbed her basket while Brice took the bucket for her. He watched her brave the chickens to feed them then grab eggs. Then they went to milk the cow. He fed the horse and the cow while she pulled on the Jersey cow. He followed her back to the house, carrying the milk. She put it all up and then followed him out to the pasture to pitch hay to the horses.

"Looks like they need some water, Brice. I'll pull the hose over and turn the water on." She grabbed the water hose and unrolled it from the wheeled carrier and then turned it on.

"Almost finished up here," Brice called down.

"Water will take a little while." She nodded and watched the troughs fill up.

Something glinted in the sun off to her left, nearly blinding her. She turned her head but couldn't find what it was. When Brice climbed down from the hay, she turned off the water and rolled the hose back up on the wheel.

A few minutes later, they started checking the garden for ripe vegetables. Halfway through the garden, she noticed a glint again. This time she asked Brice if he'd seen it.

"No, what did it look like, Ronnie?"

"It looks like something shining in the sun, like a mirror or glass of some kind. It blinded me for a second the first time, but the second time, it just was there."

"Let's go on inside, Ronnie. I don't like this." He grabbed her bucket and urged her into a fast walk. They made it inside and locked the door without incident.

"Brice, what's wrong with you?"

"I just don't want anything to happen to you. With this gang out there hunting down runaway women, I don't want to take a chance, especially without Garrett here, too."

"You didn't sound this upset about it the other night," she accused, slapping her hands on her hips.

"Believe me. I am serious about it. I just didn't see any reason to upset you. I was wrong. You need to take it very seriously." Brice checked the back window, and then the front.

Ronnie began to worry now. He wasn't acting like himself at all. She wished Garrett was there so Brice would feel more secure. He didn't seem confident that he could keep her safe. Well, she could fight just like he could. Nothing was going to happen to her. At least she hoped not.

Chapter Twelve

A knock at the door startled both of them. Brice put his finger to his mouth and pointed for her to go upstairs. Ronnie shook her head no, and he turned her around and popped her lightly on the ass. This time she did go, with a furious look in his direction. Well, she could be mad all she wanted. He wasn't taking any chances. He was glad she still had her apron on with the gun in the pocket.

When the knock came again, he crossed the room and opened the door just enough to see who it was. Two men stood outside wearing black T-shirts and sporting guns on their hips. Neither one of them looked friendly.

"What can I do for you?" he asked, still not opening the door much wider.

"You have a female here," the taller one said. He didn't ask.

"Yes, she belongs to me and my partner. Why?"

"Her description matches a runaway from back east of us. We need to see her."

"You'll just have to wait till my partner gets back. I'm not about to let you inside without us both being here."

"If she's a runaway, she comes with us."

"He'll be back late tonight. Come back tomorrow sometime." Brice kept his voice confident, as if he wasn't worried in the least.

"So you'll have time to hide her? I don't think so. Either you bring her out now, or we'll come in. There are two of us, and one of you. And," he pointed out, "we have guns."

"You'd shoot an unarmed man? Where is the justice in that?" Brice demanded.

"We are justice. If she's who we think she is, she's going back after we administer that justice."

"You mean beat her."

"She will get five licks of the whip, like all runaways get."

"And I still say you have no jurisdiction in a man's own home."

"Open the fucking door now, or I will shoot you." Until this moment the shorter man hadn't said anything.

"No, you won't, because I'll shoot you first."

Brice looked behind the two men and nearly moaned out loud. Ronnie stood behind them, but not with the gun from her pocket. She had a shotgun pointing directly at the shorter of the two men. She kept her hand steady. Brice would have sworn she was used to handling a gun. Maybe she was, but didn't like them.

The two men slowly turned around. They stared at her, and then at the gun. Brice opened the door now that there was no reason to keep it closed. He glared at her, but would save the dressing down until later, if there was a later. Garrett was going to kill him. He'd screwed up twice, where she was concerned.

"You're Rhonda Ann Sawyer," the second man said.

"I'm Ronnie. I don't go by that name anymore." She kept the gun steady on the two men.

"You are a runaway and are being sentenced to five lashes of the whip and being returned to your owner," the first man stated formally.

"I'm not going anywhere. That son of a bitch wasn't my owner. He was my jailer. No one owns me. I can live wherever I want to live, and that is here. You have no authority over me." Her voice got higher and louder as she spoke.

"You need to hand that gun to me, or I'm going to be forced to take it from you."

"Brice, move out of the way," she warned.

Brice cursed and moved to one side. She was going to shoot one of the bastards. That was all they needed. But then, he couldn't keep them from taking her, so what was his gripe?

"You take one step toward me, and I'll shoot you. Don't think I won't. At this range, I can't miss what I aim for." She lowered the gun to crotch level.

Both men froze.

* * * *

Ronnie was scared spitless, but she wasn't going back to that bastard, and they sure as hell weren't going to whip her. She might take a spanking from her guys, but she wasn't going to be whipped, hit, or slapped by another man.

"I think you want to lower that gun and come with us before you get into even more trouble, female," the shorter of the two told her.

Ronnie took a couple of steps back and to the side. She never took her aim off of their crotches, though.

"I think you need to leave now. You're not welcome on our property. Common law says I can shoot anyone trespassing on private property once it's been claimed and worked. This has been claimed and worked for three, nearly four, years now. You are trespassing. Get the fuck off."

They stood there staring at her as if she'd lost her mind. Then she racked the shotgun and they immediately backed away toward their truck sitting down at the edge of the road. She kept the gun trained on their asses until they had pulled off and were out of sight.

"Fuck, Ronnie! What in the hell do you think you were doing?" Brice grabbed the gun from her and opened it to eject the shells. Only there weren't any.

"You didn't even have it loaded," he fussed.

"I couldn't find the shells fast enough. I wasn't going to let them shoot you. They would have, Brice."

"And what in the hell are we going to do when they come back with more men? Have a damn shootout here?"

"So I'm just supposed to let them take me, whip me, and send me back to that rat bastard? I mean that little to you?"

"Hell, no, Ronnie. That's not true. I'd never have let them take you."

"Oh, you would have died for me. But you wouldn't have been able to stop them from taking me in the long run."

"Hell, there has to be something we can do, Ronnie, to stop this from happening."

Ronnie sighed and hugged him. He pulled her back into the house and locked the door. Then he leaned the shotgun up in the corner by the door before picking her up in his arms.

He sat on the couch and cradled her in his arms, smoothing one hand up and down her back.

"We'll figure something out. When Garrett gets back, we'll put our heads together and come up with something."

"If you say so, Brice. I'm tired of always having to hide."

"I know, baby." He lifted her chin and softly kissed her.

She wrapped her hands around his head and dove deeper into his kiss, opening her mouth to him. She was desperate for something to hold the fear at bay. His mouth, his body, would do just fine.

He licked along the inside of her mouth with his tongue, then explored her teeth before sucking her tongue into his mouth to tease. When he pulled back, she was about to force him down again when he nipped at her chin and nibbled his way around her jawline to her neck. He sucked and nibbled there before heading for her shoulder. He was marking her, she knew. She was fine with that. She belonged to him and Garrett, just like they belonged to her.

His hands went to the hem of her T-shirt and lifted it. When it needed to go over her head, he moved back from her shoulder and jerked it off, dropping it to the floor before returning to her collarbone. When he reached for her bra, she shoved his hands away and unhooked it herself and let it slide off. Then she grabbed at his shirt and pulled at it, trying to get it up over his head. He helped her and threw it over the back of the couch.

"I think if we're going to get anywhere fast, we're going to have to stand up for the boots and jeans," he pointed out.

Ronnie grinned and scrambled off his lap and began pulling off her boots, then worked on her jeans. She watched Brice do the same thing. When they were both naked, she jumped on him and took him down to the floor. He chuckled and swung her on top of him. She immediately worked her mouth over his chest, finding each flat disc to nibble and suck on. Then she followed the happy trail to his massive cock and enveloped the head of it in her mouth to suck.

Brice hissed out a breath and grabbed her head as she began to suck him all the way down her throat.

"Fuck!" Brice fought to pull her off of him. "I'm not going to last if you do that again. Ride me, baby."

She came off of him with an audible pop then climbed on top of him. He held his cock steady for her to slowly slide down over him. She stopped once to catch her breath at the fullness of him inside of her. When she sat flush against his pelvis, she squeezed her cunt and was rewarded with a string of curse words.

Ronnie grinned and began to slowly ride him. She used her knees to hold her as she pulled up and slammed back down again, over and over. Brice held her hips as if trying to help, but he was only holding on as she rode him to completion. When she felt him begin to come inside of her, she reached between her legs and found her clit and rubbed it. He pushed her hand out of the way and pinched it just right.

She exploded and lost her rhythm as she climaxed, clamping down on his dick as she did. He called out her name and they both collapsed against the floor. Ronnie was completely out of breath and worried she wouldn't be able to catch it again. Brice didn't sound like he was in much better shape.

After a few minutes of pulling herself together, Ronnie climbed to her feet and retrieved the shotgun. She laid it by the mattress on the floor and re-dressed in everything but her boots.

"Come on, lazy. Dress so we aren't caught with our pants down, and let's grab some sleep before Garrett makes it back home." She grabbed his limp arm and pulled him to a sitting position.

"I think sex just stirs you up. No more sex for you," Brice grumbled as he pulled on his jeans.

"I'm really worried that's going to happen. I'm going upstairs to find the damn shells to the gun and I'll be right back down." She took the stairs at a jog and realized she felt much better than she had.

Was it because of the near-disastrous episode, or because she had stood up for herself, or maybe just like Brice said, sex revved her up? No matter why, she felt good, and even though she was sleepy and could use a nap, she knew she would probably stay awake and make sure no one snuck up on them.

Deep down, Ronnie was terrified of losing her hard-won independence and the two most wonderful men she'd ever been around. She'd fight tooth and nail to stay there with them. They treated her as if she were the most precious thing in the world.

She located the shells in the drawer of the bedside table and carried them downstairs. Brice stood waiting on her, fully dressed sans boots.

"Do you know how to load it?" Brice asked.

She gave him a look and nodded. "I've been hunting for meat for the last three years. Got pretty good at it and the rifle. I just hate handguns." She expertly loaded the shotgun, then carefully laid it on the floor next to the mattress.

"Hop on, baby, and let's get some sleep. I know you've got to be tired. We both were up at the crack of dawn."

"How long before you think Garrett will be back?" she asked.

"I figure in another three, maybe four hours. He planned to be back early enough that we wouldn't have to worry about unloading in the dark. That's why he left so early." Brice pulled her into his arms. She used his shoulder as a pillow.

"I'm worried, Brice. Those men are crazy. They're not going to stop until they turn me over."

"Don't worry about it anymore now. We'll talk to Garrett and figure out what to do. Nothing is going to happen to you." He nuzzled her hair and squeezed her for a few seconds.

Ronnie shivered at the thought of being whipped. She would run again if she had to. She would miss the men because she loved them, but she wouldn't go back to the bastard who'd used her like a slave.

Chapter Thirteen

Garrett pulled up the drive at nearly five that afternoon. He was dog tired, but pleased that he had been able to find pretty much everything on the list, plus some. He hoped Ronnie would be excited at some of the things he'd managed to find for her. He had four cases of canning supplies, for one thing. Then there were the pretty shirts and blouses and skirts. He knew she wouldn't use the skirts that much, but they would be nice sometimes to wear around the house.

He backed up to the back door. Ronnie came running out with Brice right behind her, fussing. Why was he fussing at her? Garrett immediately felt the tension in the air. Something was wrong.

"Hey, you guys, what's up?" he called as he climbed out of the truck.

"Oh, we'll talk about it later after we get everything unloaded." Ronnie jumped into his arms and gave him a huge kiss. He hugged her back and kept an arm around her when she slid out of his arms.

"Brice?" Garrett asked, studying his friend for a clue.

"She's right. We should get everything unloaded before it gets dark."

"I don't think I like the sound of this." But he closed the door to the truck and walked around to open the tailgate of the truck. Ronnie squealed at the sight of the canning supplies.

"You found them! Thank you." She gave him another sloppy kiss on his cheek.

They spent the next hour and a half unloading the truck and putting things away where they went. Brice made several trips to the barn and to the shed that held the tractor and gardening supplies. Once they'd finished, Garrett went upstairs and took a shower. He was surprised and a little disappointed that Ronnie didn't join him, but figured she was too busy putting away the clothes he'd brought her. She seemed to genuinely like them. He hoped so.

After dressing again, he walked downstairs to find the two sitting at the kitchen table with a meal set up.

"Figured you needed to eat. I doubt you ate lunch," Ronnie said.

"I could definitely eat, but I want to know what is going on."

"After you eat," she said. She poured more tea in her glass.

"I'm really not liking the sounds of this."

Brice sighed and shook his head. "Nope, you're not going to."

As soon as they finished up the light meal, Garrett leaned back in the chair and gave them a *get it over with* look.

"While you were gone, the gang looking for runaway females showed up." Brice said it quick.

It took a few seconds for it to sink in. Then it hit him. Fuck! He immediately reached across and took Ronnie's hand.

"What happened?"

"They wanted Ronnie, but I refused to let them see her."

"They were going to shoot Brice for not letting them in, so I grabbed the shotgun and ran around the house and cornered them with it." Ronnie looked proud of herself.

"You did what?" he demanded.

"Yeah, she did. She told them she would shoot them if they didn't leave, and then leveled the gun at their balls." Brice took a sip of his tea.

"What would you have done if they had called you on it, Ronnie?"

"Shot their freaking balls off. I'm not going back, and they sure as hell aren't going to whip me."

"Ah, hell, Ronnie. There's no way we'll let them take you." Garrett grabbed her hand and squeezed it. He looked over at Brice and caught the worry in his eyes.

"What are you going to do then? They'll be back, and they'll have more men with them," Ronnie pointed out.

"Possession is nine-tenths of the law, Ronnie."

"There is no law. That's why these crazies can do this. There's no one to stop them."

"There's us now," Brice suggested.

"There's us," Garrett agreed. "Look, the entire thing is about ownership. They say this guy owned you. Did he have papers to say he owned you?"

"No. He didn't own me. You can't own a human being anymore." Ronnie frowned.

"Now, you can. They buy and sell females in Border Town all the time. They issue bills of sale. It's proof of ownership." Garrett looked over at Brice for confirmation. He'd been out most recently in that area.

"That's true. You buy a female, or trade for one, you are given a certificate of ownership." He looked thoughtful. "So what you're suggesting is that we draw up a bill of sale or certificate of ownership of her?"

"Hell no! No one owns me," she all but growled.

"It wouldn't mean anything to us, baby, but it would mean something to them, and they would leave you alone," Brice told her.

"You're both serious about this, aren't you?" she demanded.

"Ronnie, we have to keep you safe, and if this is all it takes, then what's the big deal? We know better. Why does it matter if anyone else thinks differently?" Garrett asked.

"It doesn't. I just hate the idea that there's a piece of paper that has my name on it as belonging to someone. Even if it is you two." She sighed and rubbed her face with her hands.

"Let's get to work, Brice. They'll be back soon, I'm sure."

"How well do you write?" Garrett asked Brice.

"Probably not well enough to make it look professional. I've always had bad handwriting."

"Hell, mine is probably worse. My big hands never held a pencil very well." Garrett sighed, holding out his hands.

"Get some damn paper and a pen. I'll write the thing out. I used to do calligraphy." She sniffed and brushed away a tear.

Garrett got up and wrapped his arms around her. "It's going to be okay, baby. I promise."

"That's easy for you to say. You don't have to have *owners* to be safe."

"Here you go, Ronnie." Brice handed her several pieces of paper and a pen.

"Let me mess with it, and then you can look at it. Go on and leave me alone," she fussed.

"Come on, Brice. We'll do chores. We can see if anyone comes up from the barn." Garrett grabbed the milk bucket and handed it to Brice, who frowned. "Sorry man, I can't do it. Big hands, you know."

As soon as they were outside, Garrett cornered Brice. "Is that all that happened? They didn't touch her, did they?"

"No, they never got close enough to, but they had been watching us all morning, evidently." He told Garrett about the glint Ronnie had seen twice before they went inside.

"If this doesn't work, I'm moving her farther west. Are you coming with us?" Garrett asked.

"Hell yeah, I'm coming. I'd already thought about that. I figured we would go on the other side of Sky Line, maybe a little farther north."

"Good idea. The southwest area is pretty much dead, from what we've seen in the past," Garrett agreed.

"Best thing to do would be to load up and leave in the middle of the night. We'd have to open all the gates and let the animals out, but they'd make it." Brice set up the stool and sat down to milk the cow.

"I'm going to go put up the chickens so I can watch the house while you milk." Garrett left Brice struggling to milk the cow.

Brice walked out with a half-full bucket of milk and a pained expression on his face. Garrett frowned.

"What's wrong?"

"My fucking hands are cramping."

Garrett struggled not to laugh at his friend. Brice must have been able to tell, because he scowled at him. He followed him into the house, staying well away from the swinging bucket of milk.

"Ronnie?" Garrett called as soon as they walked inside.

"I'm right here."

Her voice came from the kitchen area. He slipped off his boots and peeked around the door of the laundry/utility room. She sat at the kitchen table with several pieces of paper strewn around in front of her. He could hear the tears in her voice.

"I'll be right there, baby. I'm going to wash my hands." He turned on the water in the utility sink and cornered Brice before he could walk in. "She's upset. Let her be for a few minutes."

"I'll just stick the milk in the cellar then come back up and wash my hands," he whispered back.

He disappeared down the stairs leading to the cellar as Garrett walked into the kitchen. He could see her bent over the table, but she wasn't doing anything. He wanted to go to her but figured she needed a few seconds to calm down. No doubt she'd been crying all the time they were outside.

"You might as well come on over and have a seat. I'm not going to calm down anytime soon," she finally groused.

Garrett walked up behind her and bent over and kissed the top of her head, then wrapped his arms around her shoulders and hugged her. She leaned back into his arms. It felt good to know she felt safe with him. A few seconds later, Brice walked in and looked at them. He lifted an eyebrow as if to ask if it was okay to come in. Garrett just nodded.

"We got everything done, so we're ready to call it a night whenever you are, Ronnie." Brice took a seat across from her.

Garrett leaned over and tilted her chin upward so he could kiss her. He gave her a gentle, loving kiss. No tongue, all lips, and plenty of emotion. Then he looked at the papers scattered around the table and blinked.

They looked like original bills of sale. Yet they were more than that. They were works of art. She'd written the sale up, and then decorated around it as if it were a certificate or something. They looked so real he had a hard time believing they weren't.

"My God!" Brice said, staring at the papers as well. "They're perfect, but, baby, we only need one."

"I couldn't get it right. If I was going to sell myself, I wanted it to be perfect, and I can't get it right."

Garrett walked around to the other side of the table and sat down, but he took hold of her hand. He took the pen out of her hand and sat it down.

"Ronnie, they're all works of art. Let me show you what I'm going to do. I'm going to put one of these in our files we have up in the bedroom and the other one, I'm going to fold it up and put it in my billfold so I'll always have you with me."

"Oh, Garrett. That's so sappy." She giggled through the tears.

It was what he wanted, to see her smile again. He knew this was tough on her, but they didn't have a choice unless they moved, and that still wasn't out of the question yet.

"You're sure it will be okay?" she asked.

"It says exactly what it needs to say, baby," Brice told her.

"Okay, I think I'm going to take a bath and then go to bed. I'm really tired." She stood up and headed toward the stairs.

"I'll bring up a bucket of hot water for you," Garrett called out.

He grabbed one of the buckets and filled it with water before sitting it on the stove and turning it on high.

"I'm going to put one of these in my wallet as well. I feel like a bastard with it, though," Brice confessed.

"I do, too, but I also like knowing it's there because it means no one is going to take her away from us."

"We hope." Brice folded up the bill of sale and stuck it in his wallet. Then he took all the other evidence of her work and walked into the other room.

"What are you doing?" Garrett asked as he followed Brice.

"I'm going to burn these so no one knows she made them." He threw the wadded-up mess into the fireplace, then set a match to it.

Garrett watched it burn with Brice. Then he went and checked the water on the stove. It seemed warm enough for a hot summer night, so he carted it upstairs for Ronnie's bath.

He found her sitting in the cold water with her legs drawn up to her chin. She looked up and smiled at him.

"Watch the toes, it's hot," he warned her as he slowly added the water to the bath. "Do I need to slow down?"

"Nope, it feels good. Thanks, Garrett. I'm sorry I'm being such a baby about this. It just hurts to know that I'm just a piece of meat to men now."

"Honey, I prefer to think of you as a beautiful woman whom I love very much and who means the world to me. You are more precious than anything I have ever owned. I feel privileged to be allowed to take care of you."

She smiled again and reached for him. He knelt beside the tub and leaned in to kiss her. Ronnie curled her hands into his hair and pulled him closer so that their foreheads met. She took his lips with a kiss then sucked his bottom lip inside of her mouth. He groaned as she ran her tongue all around it.

When she pulled away he felt the loss. Garrett leaned back on his knees and watched as she leaned back in the tub and closed her eyes.

"Garrett?"

"Yeah, baby?"

"I want you and Brice to make love to me tonight—together."

"You know we'd love to, Ronnie, but why tonight?" he asked.

"Because if you are going to own me, I want to feel both of you inside of me, possessing me."

"Aw, honey. We love you so much. Don't let this change how you feel about us or yourself. You're no different than you ever are."

"I know, but I need you, both of you, with me tonight."

"We'll take good care of you. Want me to scrub your back?" he asked.

"Naw, I'm just going to soak for a while."

Garrett stood up and started to walk away, but she stopped him.

"Take the lamp with you, Garrett. I want to soak in the dark. It feels so peaceful like this."

"I'm afraid you'll fall when you get out, baby."

"I won't. Please?"

"Only if you promise to call one of us to come get you with the lamp when you're ready to come downstairs." Garrett waited for her to answer him.

"Okay, I promise."

"Good girl. I'll be in the living room waiting on you."

Garrett took one last look at her beautiful body soaking in the tub and wished he could give her what she wanted more than anything in the world, her freedom.

Chapter Fourteen

Ronnie felt so much more relaxed by the time the water grew cool. She sat up then climbed out of the tub in the dark. She held on to the counter and searched for her towel. Once she'd found it, she dried off and slipped on the sandals she had brought in the bathroom with her. She had promised Garrett she would call when she was ready to come down. Part of her wanted to rebel, but the other part of her reminded her that it wasn't their fault, and they really didn't see her as a possession.

She drew in a couple of deep breaths and let them out slowly. She needed to put it behind her because she was upsetting the men. She walked to the edge of the bathroom and called out.

"I'm ready whenever someone wants to come get me."

"I'll be right up," Brice's voice called back.

She smiled to herself. Brice would insist on holding her hand. Of course, Garrett would probably have carried her down. He liked holding her like that. The truth be known, she liked it when he held her. She felt safe. She liked to hold Brice's hand. She felt loved.

"There you are." Brice was totally naked carrying the lamp. "You ready to go downstairs, or did you need anything in the bedroom first?"

"I'm ready."

They walked down the stairs together with Brice holding her hand. When they arrived in the living room, Garrett was also nude and had changed the sheets on the bed on the floor. He had two lamps lit around the room so that it fairly glowed a golden hue.

"It's pretty with the lamps on like this."

"I thought so, too. Plus, I want to see you when you come," Garrett confessed.

"Lay back on the mattress, baby," Brice instructed.

She relaxed back on the mattress and waited for whatever they decided to do next. She felt safe in their hands. She knew they would never hurt her or allow anyone to hurt her.

Brice shouldered his way between her legs and blew across her pussy. It was damp already from just the thought of taking both of them into her body at one time. Garrett had played with her plenty of times, but never fucked her in the ass before. She was a little scared, but mostly of the unknown.

"You're so beautiful, Ronnie," Garrett told her as he lay down next to her.

He reached over and brushed the back of his hand across her nipples. She shivered, unable to stop it. The sensation traveled all over her body. When he leaned in and licked across one of them she moaned. Brice chose that moment to lick her pussy lips. She shivered again and knew this was going to be one of those times she was going to come apart when they took her.

She swallowed as Brice spread her cunt wide and tongued her deeply. He licked her from top to bottom and then delved inside of her with his tongue stiffened like a cock. She moaned. Brice inserted two fingers and began finger-fucking her. When he licked over her clit, she reached down to grab his head and hold him there, but Garrett held her back.

"No, baby. Let him have you. I want these pretty breasts where I can get to them." He pulled on her nipples until she lifted her chest to relieve some of the pull. It didn't really hurt, just burned.

He leaned in then and sucked on the offended nipple until she was lifting her breast again to try and shove more of her tit into his mouth. He released that nipple only to go and suck in the other one. Ronnie wanted to scream for him to pinch them, bite them, do something. He was only teasing her, and she wasn't in the mood for teasing. She wanted action.

Brice surprised her by stroking his fingers over her G-spot. She hissed out a *yes* in pleasure as he did it again and again. Then he stopped and sucked her pussy lips into his mouth and teased them with his tongue.

"Please, someone fuck me. I can't stand all this teasing. I want to come."

"Patience, baby," Brice said with a smile in his voice. "We want this to be good for you."

"It's good, it's good. Please," she repeated.

Garrett twisted her nipple and bit on the other one. She moaned and bowed her back at the pleasure-pain that suffused her body.

"Brice, she's ready for more." Garrett stretched out beside her.

"Just a minute, Garrett. I have to feel her come on my face."

Ronnie whimpered in need at this. She wanted to come no matter how she did it. She tried to tilt her pelvis to rub her clit over Brice's face. He chuckled and placed a hand on her pelvis to keep her still.

The sensation of his tongue licking all around her clit without touching it drove her crazy. She was crying now, she was in so much need.

"Please, Brice."

He curled his fingers and stroked heavily over her hot spot as he nipped at her clit, sending red-hot shards of electricity coursing through her body all at once. She screamed and came so hard she thought her ears would explode with ringing.

"That's it, baby. Give me that sweet cum." Brice licked her cunt over and over, only making her climax go on and on until she tried to pull him away from her.

"Climb over on top of me, baby," Garrett said. He helped her roll over and away from Brice's questing tongue.

She climbed over him and lowered herself onto his thick cock an inch at a time. He was so large, she couldn't just plop down without giving her body time to adjust. She moaned as she slowly took him in. His eyes closed and he threw his head back as she engulfed him in her hot cunt made slick with her pussy juices.

Once she had taken all of him in, she began to move up and down on his dick. She couldn't be still. He felt too good inside of her. She loved being filled. After a few seconds of fucking Garrett, Brice pushed down on her back until she was lying on top of Garrett. He kissed both cheeks of her ass before laying two swift swats to them. She groaned. It sent shivers down her back with Garrett's cock inside of her.

Brice squeezed something on her ass that was cold and felt like jelly. She knew it would be lube. He rubbed it around her back hole, then slowly pushed inward as she pushed out. His finger popped in without any trouble. He pushed it all the way to the last knuckle, then pulled it back, out only to do it again. He did this several times before adding a second finger. She felt this one burn a bit when he pushed through her tight ring. Then he was fucking her with them all the way up to his knuckles. He slid them in and out over and over again. Finally, he pulled them out and squeezed more lube inside of her before fitting the head of his cock at her back door.

Ronnie knew it would hurt at first, but she wasn't prepared for the burn. She cried out, and he stopped.

"Push out, Ronnie. It will only burn for a few seconds if you push out."

He began to push in again, and this time she took a deep breath and pushed out. He popped inside of her and stopped to let her adjust. She panted until Garrett took her mouth with a kiss. He whispered sweet words in her ear until she began to breathe easier.

"There you go, baby," Brice said. He pulled out a little ways then pushed in again, gaining ground as he did. Over and over he pulled out and pushed in until he was all the way inside of her.

Ronnie moaned when he began slowly to fuck her. As he pulled out, Garrett pushed farther in. Then they switched, and while Brice pushed in, Garrett pulled out. She couldn't do anything but lie there and let them control the pace. She was helpless to do anything. All she could do was feel. Nerve endings in her ass came alive. The push and pull between the men rubbed her in so many different places that normally didn't get stimulated. She felt crammed full of cock.

"Oh, God. This feels so good," she finally managed to get out.

"What do you need, baby?" Brice asked in a strained voice.

"I need you to move faster, harder, something. I'm on fire."

They picked up the pace, and soon she was slamming down on Garrett then pushing back on Brice as hard as she could. The burn was more pleasure than she thought she could handle. Much more and she would die. They pummeled her over and over in every part of her body. When she thought she would explode, Brice reached around and pinched her clit between his finger and thumb and sent her spiraling out of control. She screamed as she came harder than she ever had.

Somewhere in the back of her head, she knew they had come as well, but for a few brief seconds, she couldn't think, or see, or hear. For a brief moment, she must have passed out, because the last thing she remembered was that the room seemed to be glowing around her.

* * * *

"Is she okay?" Brice asked, worried when she didn't answer them.

"She's fine. She passed out. We done good, Brice." Garrett grinned.

Brice wasn't so sure. He needed her to wake up and say something.

"Why are you both staring at me like that?"

"You passed out. I was worried." Brice leaned in and kissed her.

They were all lying on the mattress on the floor. Garrett had cleaned her up while Brice had cleaned up, and now they were lying there over her, watching her. She looked fine, he decided. Since when had he become the worrier, while Garrett was the more secure one?

"That was wonderful. I never knew it could be like that."

"You were wonderful," Brice told her. "You can't imagine what that feels like to us."

"I felt so connected to both of you at the same time. I loved it. I felt whole," Ronnie whispered up to them.

"I love you, baby," Garrett told her and kissed her lightly on the lips.

"I love you, too." She reached for his hand. Then she reached for Brice's. "I love you, Brice."

"I love you, Ronnie. More than anything in this world." He squeezed her hand.

They rolled over and spooned despite the heat in the house. Ronnie couldn't remember ever feeling so loved and cared for. She thought she would fall asleep almost immediately but found she was awake long after the men had begun to snore.

She realized she was worried about when the men would come back to get her. She couldn't help but wonder if they would even listen to Garrett and Brice when they said they owned her. That word stuck in her mind. She hated it, but in order for her to be safe, they had to own her.

She thought about the world and all that had happened to her over the years. Nothing had prepared her for New America and her lot in life as an owned female of two men. Still, she wouldn't trade places with anyone right now. She loved them, and they her. She was where she needed and wanted to be. If only the gang would leave them alone.

Somewhere in the middle of the night, she drifted off to sleep with thoughts of growing old with her two men floating in her head.

The next morning, they got up and dressed as if nothing was wrong in their world. She gathered the eggs and milked the cow, but Brice stuck by her like a bodyguard while Garrett fed the animals.

Then they all worked in the garden picking beans, tomatoes, squash, okra, corn, and peas. Once inside, she put them to work cleaning corn while she shelled peas and beans. They waited until it cooled down to put the vegetables up, since having the stove on only heated the house up more.

This was their routine over the next few days. Always, the threat of the gang coming back hung over them. It wore on Ronnie enough that she lost her appetite and had to be coaxed to eat. She just wished they would come on and get it over with. Was it their plan to lure them into feeling safe and then just snatch her? She didn't know what to believe now.

Finally, late one evening, a truck pulled up into their drive with four men in it. They got out and slowly walked to the front of the house.

Ronnie saw them from the garden and ran to the house where the men were already cutting up corn.

"They're here. They just got out of the truck up front."

"Come on, it's going to be fine, baby." Brice pulled her into his arms.

They walked into the house and for once, didn't take off their boots but walked straight into the living room with them on. Just as they made it to the door, someone knocked. Brice held her close to him as Garrett walked over and unlocked the door. He opened it, blocking it from their view with his big body.

"What can I do for you?" he asked.

"You've got my woman here, and I want her back."

Ronnie nearly passed out. It was Carl. How in the hell had he gotten here? She was lost. They would take her from Brice and Garrett. She began to shake.

"We need the female, please," one of the men said.

"She's not his female. Does he have a bill of sale?" Garrett asked.

"I don't need a bill of sale. She's mine." Carl's voice sounded even whinier than what she remembered.

"Without a bill of sale dated after ours, you can't have her."

"Do you have a bill of sale, sir?" one of the men asked.

"I sure do." Garrett dug in his back pocket and pulled out his wallet. He pulled out her paper and unfolded it. He handed it to someone.

"Looks in order to me, Sam. What do you think?"

"Yep, looks like Clemmie's work. They probably bought her from Clemmie," the other man said.

Garrett fiddled with his wallet then put it back in his back pocket. "Does this stop this mess of harassing us?"

"You have a bill of sale for her, and this man doesn't. Without a bill of sale dated after yours, he doesn't have ownership rights."

"Like hell! She's mine. I had her back before they even knew her. She's mine, I tell you."

"Sir, you're going to have to leave this area. If you return for any reason, we will be forced to escort you, and that will lead to a penalty."

"Penalty? You're threatening me?" Carl demanded.

"Just telling you the truth. Let's go."

Garrett stepped back from the door to close it, but not before Carl caught sight of Ronnie.

He lunged for her and nearly had his hands on her, but Garrett stopped him with a fist to the gut. The scrawny man bent double, gasping for breath.

"You ever try and touch our woman again, I'll kill you. Do you understand me?" Garrett asked him.

Carl couldn't do anything but nod. The three men who'd come with him grabbed him by the collar and hauled him out of the house and back toward the truck. One of them turned around and looked at them. He stared at them a long time then climbed into the truck, and it pulled out of their drive.

"It's over," Brice said.

"It's over," Garrett agreed.

"But we're not," Ronnie said with tears in her eyes.

"No, we're just getting started." Garrett pulled her into his arms and kissed her while Brice hugged her from behind.

THE END

WWW.MARLAMONROE.COM

ABOUT THE AUTHOR

Marla Monroe lives in the southern part of the United States. She writes sexy romance from the heart and often puts a twist of suspense in her books. She is a nurse and works in a busy hospital, but finds plenty of time to follow her two passions, reading and writing. You can find her in a book store or a library at any given time when she's not at work or writing. Marla would love for you to visit her at her blog at themarlamonroe.blogspot.com and leave a comment. You can also reach her at themarlamonroe@yahoo.com

Also by Marla Monroe

Ménage Everlasting: Men of the Border Lands 1: *Belonging to Them*
Ménage Everlasting: Men of the Border Lands 2: *A Home with Them*
Ménage Everlasting: Men of the Border Lands 4:
Their Bartered Bride

For all other titles, please visit
www.BookStrand.com/Marla-Monroe

Siren Publishing, Inc.
www.SirenPublishing.com

Lightning Source UK Ltd.
Milton Keynes UK
UKHW02f1445070318
319039UK00006B/945/P

9 781